A DREAM ROLE

"*Nutcracker on Ice,* a nationally televised Christmas special,'" Jill read out loud. "'Auditions at Seneca Hills. Junior skaters are eligible for the starring role of Clara.'"

Here she was, working hard to prove she was ready to go back to the Ice Academy. What could be more perfect than this? A starring role in an ice-skating spectacular, with world-famous skaters, on television!

I've just got to get that role, Jill told herself as she stared at the poster. No matter how hard it is, no matter how much work it takes—I'm going to skate Clara. I'm the best in Silver Blades. I just know I can do it! After all, who could stop me?

Other Skylark Books you will enjoy
Ask your bookseller for the books you have missed

Anne of Green Gables by L. M. Montgomery

The Great Mom Swap by Betsy Haynes

The Great Dad Disaster by Betsy Haynes

Horse Crazy, The Saddle Club #1
by Bonnie Bryant

Seal Child by Sylvia Peck

The Wild Mustang by Joanna Campbell

Spell It M-U-R-D-E-R by Ivy Ruckman

Pronounce It Dead by Ivy Ruckman

Elvis Is Back, and He's in the Sixth Grade!
by Stephen Mooser

What Is the Teacher's Toupee Doing in the Fish Tank?
by Jerry Piasecki

THE BIG
AUDITION

Melissa Lowell

Created by Parachute Press

A SKYLARK BOOK
NEW YORK · TORONTO · LONDON · SYDNEY · AUCKLAND

With special thanks to Darlene Parent, director of Sky Rink Skating School, New York City.

RL 5.2, 009–012

THE BIG AUDITION
A Skylark Book / November 1995

Skylark Books is a registered trademark of Bantam Books, a division of Bantam Doubleday Dell Publishing Group, Inc. Registered in U.S. Patent and Trademark Office and elsewhere.

ISBN 0-553-48349-8

Published simultaneously in the United States and Canada

Bantam Books are published by Bantam Books, a division of Bantam Doubleday Dell Publishing Group, Inc. Its trademark, consisting of the words "Bantam Books" and the portrayal of a rooster, is Registered in U.S. Patent and Trademark Office and in other countries. Marca Registrada. Bantam Books, 1540 Broadway, New York, New York 10036.

PRINTED IN THE UNITED STATES OF AMERICA

OPM   0 9 8 7 6 5 4 3 2 1

1

Jill Wong came out of a perfect flying camel with a scratch spin. She skidded to a full stop. Pleased with herself, she glanced up. And frowned. Across the rink, a girl who had been staring at her half an hour ago still had her eyes on Jill.

Jill shook her head, annoyed with herself. After all, she was used to people watching her skate. She was a member of Silver Blades, one of the best competitive figure-skating clubs in the United States, and she was one of the best skaters in the club.

She had been skating with Silver Blades since she was eight years old—younger than the girl who was watching her now, she guessed. And after all those years Jill had gotten used to being stared at. Skaters were performers. Whether they were at practice sessions or in competition, someone was always watching them closely. You just had to learn to concentrate and ignore it.

But there was something about the way this girl was watching her that made Jill uncomfortable. At first she couldn't figure out what it was. The girl must have been about ten or eleven years old, with light brown hair and a slim body. She looked ordinary enough. But there was nothing ordinary in the way she was staring at Jill.

That's it! Jill thought. That's what's wrong. The girl wasn't watching Jill as if she admired her, as so many younger skaters did. This girl was staring at Jill as if she was *judging* her. And finding something wrong with Jill's every move.

Well, let her look, Jill told herself. I have nothing to worry about. I'm skating really well!

Jill tossed her long black braid behind one shoulder and moved into the flying camel again. She was feeling particularly strong this morning. And confident. No matter what any ten-year-old might think, Jill knew she was good. Very good.

So good that the year before, Jill had been chosen to train at the prestigious International Ice Academy in Denver, Colorado. It was a great honor—and a lot of hard work. But Jill loved it. She would still be at the Academy if it hadn't been for the accident.

It had happened when Jill was home on vacation. She had gone hiking with her new boyfriend, Ryan McKensey. Ryan was fifteen and her first real boyfriend. Jill had been thirteen then and a little nervous that Ryan and his friends wouldn't accept her. But they were impressed that Jill was a figure skater. So Jill had started showing off for them, leaping from rock to rock on the hiking trail. Then Jill took a bad fall and broke her left foot.

She still remembered how tough it had been to call Ludmila Petrova, the co-owner of the Academy, to tell her about the accident. Ludmila hadn't made it easy for Jill. She only said that Jill should stay in touch and let them know when she was ready to skate competitively again. So Jill had stayed home in Seneca Hills and gone back to her old school.

Jill's foot had been in a cast for two long months. And then there were more weeks of physical therapy. For a while Jill was afraid that she'd never skate again. But finally she had been allowed back on the ice. Since that time Jill had worked extra hard to get back into shape—because she had a goal. All she wanted, all she could think about, was getting strong enough to impress Ludmila. She just *had* to go back to the Ice Academy. And she would, too.

Jill came out of the flying camel with the scratch spin again.

"Way to go!" Jill's coach, Kathy Bart, gave her a thumbs-up sign. "You were really focused, and it showed. Now, let's run through the whole program. Then we'll call it a day."

Jill grinned with pride. Kathy was a great coach. She was pretty strict, and she could be tough—so tough that the girls had nicknamed her Sarge, though they never called her that to her face. But Kathy was also fair, and she never failed to give Jill praise when she had earned it.

Jill took a deep breath to clear her mind. Focus, she reminded herself.

She struck the opening pose for her program. Then she began to power around the rink in long, clean crossovers. She built up speed, then stepped into a single axel, keeping her left leg crossed over her right. After one and a half rotations in the air, she landed solidly on her right skate. That was the easy part.

The next move was the camel spin. Carefully Jill transferred her weight to her left foot—the one that had been broken.

"Stop babying that foot!" Kathy called.

Jill flushed, embarrassed that Kathy had caught her. Her foot was healed now. Jill couldn't afford to baby it or even to think about it while she skated. It took away her concentration, and a skater had to concentrate at all times.

Keeping her right leg back, Jill was careful to keep her chin up and her arms straight, and to spin at an even pace. Now came the most difficult part of Jill's routine. She had to land a double axel on her right skate and finish with a flying camel.

The toughest part is in my mind, Jill reminded herself. If I *want* to do it, I can.

She rounded the far end of the rink again. As she did she noticed the girl who'd been staring at her whisper something to a tall, slim woman standing next to her.

Her mother, Jill guessed. As Jill skated past them the girl pointed at Jill. Then, just as Jill was about to go for her double axel, the girl did an exact imitation of the camel spin that Jill had just completed—only she wobbled her left ankle as she started the move.

Jill gasped. She couldn't believe it! Had her ankle really wobbled like that? And even if it had, how could anyone be so mean as to make fun of her?

In the split second before Jill brought her arms in tight to her body, she overrotated her shoulders. Before she knew it, she had lost her balance. *Thwack!* Jill fell hard onto the ice.

"Ouch!" She winced in pain, then pulled herself up, brushing ice from her red wool tights. Now the girl was staring at her openly. As Jill watched, the girl even giggled.

Jill felt a flare of anger as she skated over to Kathy. She knew she couldn't make excuses. Kathy would only tell Jill she was experienced enough not to be distracted by anyone.

"Sorry," Jill mumbled. "I lost my concentration."

"Yes," Kathy replied, "I saw that. Do it again, Jill. And this time, focus."

Jill was determined not to mess up a second time. She glided onto center ice and took a deep breath, closing her eyes and thinking only about her program. She skated cleanly through the whole routine and ended by landing her double axel perfectly.

I nailed it, she told herself with satisfaction. As she

left the ice she glanced across the rink, hoping the girl had seen her skate. But she was gone. Jill felt annoyed again.

"Good work, Jill," Kathy called. "See you tomorrow."

Jill waved good-bye. Then she slipped on her skate guards and headed into the locker room. Two of her friends, Nikki Simon and Haley Arthur, looked up as Jill entered.

"Hey, Jill," Nikki greeted her. "How's it going?" Nikki was a pairs skater. She had moved to Seneca Hills only two years ago, but Jill had felt close to Nikki from the start. When Jill was away at the Ice Academy, Nikki had written her the most letters of all her friends from Silver Blades.

Nikki had wavy brown hair and green eyes. That day she was wearing a red turtleneck top that Jill hadn't seen before.

"Great top, Nikki," Jill said. "Is it new?"

"Yeah," Nikki answered. "I thought about you as soon as I saw it." She smiled. Everyone knew that red was Jill's favorite color. She used to wear it every day, though lately Jill was wearing other colors as well.

"Well, red looks great on you, too," Jill told Nikki.

Nikki smiled with pleasure. "Thanks. It's an early Christmas present."

"Christmas!" Haley wailed. "Don't even *talk* to me about Christmas!" Haley was another pairs skater. She had a style all her own. She usually dressed in baggy jeans and oversized T-shirts. With her curly red hair and the single earring she always wore, Haley made a lasting impression.

"I've been so busy with skating and schoolwork," Haley continued, "I can't even think about a major holiday! How will I ever get my Christmas shopping done?"

"Oh, Haley," Nikki teased her gently. "You always worry. But you always get everything done, too."

"Not this time," Haley began to say. Just then the door to the locker room swung open and two more of Jill's friends burst in.

Martina Nemo had shoulder-length dark hair and beautiful dark eyes. Her black turtleneck sweater complemented her clear olive skin. Martina was a singles skater. She was talented and a hard worker, but she didn't yet have the technical skill that Jill had.

Martina was with Tori Carsen, another singles skater. With her blond hair, blue eyes, and lovely figure, Tori looked very mature for her age. She was pretty, and she was also a tough and very competitive athlete.

In fact, Jill and Tori were always trying to outdo each other on the ice. Their rivalry had caused some problems, but Jill knew it had also made each of them a better skater.

"Hey, what's wrong?" Haley asked when she saw the expression on Tori's face.

"It's Mr. Weiler," Tori explained. "He cut our practice short." Tori turned to Jill. "He's never done that before."

"Did he tell you why?" Jill asked.

"He said he had an upset stomach," Tori answered. "But that's not such a big deal. Not something you'd stop a whole practice session for. I don't get it."

"He must have had a reason, Tori," Jill said. Tori was a great skater and a loyal friend, but she could be a little insensitive.

Martina nodded. "Even coaches get sick, you know."

"Yeah, but not Mr. Weiler." Tori began changing out of her black and pink velvet skating dress. "I mean, even when he's had a bad cold or something, he's *never* canceled."

"Maybe you should get him something," Jill suggested. "My mom always gives me flat soda when my stomach's upset."

"Good idea," Martina agreed. "When we've finished changing, let's see if he's in his office."

"Okay," Tori agreed.

"Well, good luck," Jill said. She grabbed her red parka and her skate bag and started to push open the locker room door. "Hey—what's this?" Jill stopped dead in her tracks.

On the back of the door, facing her, was a huge poster that hadn't been there before. It said AUDITIONS in big block letters across the top.

"You guys," Jill called. "Take a look at this!" She read the poster quickly. "I don't believe it!" she exclaimed.

"Don't believe what?" Haley ran up beside her.

" '*Nutcracker on Ice,*' " Jill read out loud. " 'Auditions at Seneca Hills Ice Arena.' " She turned to her friends.

"Auditions for *The Nutcracker*—and it's going to be on television! That's my very favorite Christmas story! I've read the book about a dozen times. And I've seen the ballet, too. It'll be a great ice show!"

Tori pulled on her sneakers and hurried over. "Let me see. What's this about television?"

"It's all right here," Jill said. "A nationally televised Christmas special. Starring Christopher Kane as the Nutcracker Prince and Trisha McCoy as the Sugarplum Fairy!"

"Wow, they're my favorite skaters!" Martina quickly finished brushing her hair and came to look at the poster. "I can't believe we could actually skate with them!"

"But what about the auditions?" Tori said impatiently.

"Here it is," Jill told her, stooping down to read the print at the bottom. " 'Roles available for singles and pairs skaters. Junior skaters are eligible for the starring role of Clara. Other roles include party guests, mice, snowflakes, and flowers.' "

"Mice? Ick," Tori said, wrinkling her nose. "Who'd want to be a mouse?"

"No, you don't understand," Jill said. Her eyes were shining with excitement. "The mice have some great parts. Don't you know the story?"

Tori shook her head.

"It's wonderful," Jill told her. "This girl, Clara, gets a nutcracker for Christmas. Only it's not really a nutcracker. It's a prince who's under a magic spell. Clara breaks the spell and the prince comes alive. He rescues her from the evil Mouse King, and then they go off to the Land of Sweets together. In the ballet, all the roles have lots of impressive jumps and spins."

Martina nodded. "If it's good enough for Kane and McCoy, it's good enough for me!"

"Me too," Jill said. "It says the show will be taped in Boston on December twenty-third. Show coordinators are traveling the country searching for local talent." Jill looked up in surprise. "The scouts will be here in two weeks," she cried.

"Not much time," Martina remarked.

"But it's a great opportunity." Tori looked thoughtful. "National TV. Incredible."

Jill nodded slowly. It *was* incredible, all right. Here she was, working hard to prove she was ready to go back to the Ice Academy. What could be more perfect than this? A starring role in an ice-skating spectacular, with world-famous skaters, on television!

If Jill could skate Clara on national TV, everyone in the country would see her. They would *have* to offer her a place at the Academy again. She could even go back as a skating star!

I've just *got* to get that role, Jill told herself as she stared at the poster. No matter how hard it is, no matter how much work it takes—I'm going to skate Clara. I'm the best in Silver Blades. I just know I can do it! After all, who could stop me?

2

"Move over, Jill!" Jill's five-year-old twin brothers, Michael and Mark, crowded close to her on the bed. Jill's sister Kristi, who was nine, plopped down next to Jill on the other side. Seven-year-old Randi squeezed in next to Kristi and peered over Jill's shoulder.

"Wait for me, Jill." Henry, who was eleven, hurried into the bedroom and sat down on the rug at Jill's feet.

"Okay, you guys, settle down." Jill smiled. Having a big family could be a pain, but during the holidays it was really nice.

Jill opened the big picture book on her lap. Everyone leaned closer to see. Reading *The Nutcracker* at Christmas time was a Wong family tradition. But this year it seemed extra special. This time when Jill read the story, she'd be thinking about how to play Clara in the ice show.

Jill cleared her throat. " 'Once upon a time there was a little girl named Clara who lived with her mother and her father and her brother, Fritz,' " she began.

As she read, a delicious smell wafted up the hallway and through the house. Jill's father was downstairs in the kitchen making his famous holiday chocolate chip cookies. The Wong family was definitely getting into the Christmas spirit.

Just as Jill finished the story Mrs. Wong popped her head in the door.

"Okay, everybody," she said. "Milk and cookies downstairs! Then it's time for pj's and teeth-brushing."

"Milk and cookies!" Michael and Mark exclaimed together. "Milk and cookies!" They charged out of the room. Kristi and Randi leaped off the bed and followed them.

"They're all so cute," Mrs. Wong said to Jill. She put an arm around Jill's shoulders as they went downstairs.

"I know," Jill responded with a smile. "I really missed them when I was away at the Academy."

Mrs. Wong stopped on the stairs for a moment. "I know you've been thinking about the Academy a lot, sweetheart. And you've been working so hard on your skating. I have a feeling you're going to get your Christmas wish." She smiled. "Would that be a ticket to Colorado, maybe?"

Jill blushed a little and gave her mother a hug. "Maybe. Oh, Mom, if only I could get to play Clara! I know it would help get me back into the Academy. I really hope I get the role!"

"I do, too, sweetheart." Her mother gave Jill another quick hug. "Now, let's see what those kids are doing to your father. With those cookies around, it could get dangerous."

"Really!" Jill agreed, giggling.

Downstairs, they found Mr. Wong sitting on the living room couch surrounded by children. Henry struggled to hold two-year-old Laurie on his knees. Laurie laughed and bounced, clutching a cookie in each of her pudgy hands.

Mrs. Wong took Laurie in her arms. "Thank you, Henry," she said. "But get some cookies yourself before they're all gone. You too, Jill."

Jill grabbed a couple of cookies from the plate and reached to pour herself some milk. Just then Michael and Mark began to wrestle over the last cookie. They bumped into the table, and Jill's milk spilled all over her. She leaped up.

"You guys!" Jill yelled. "You never watch where you're going." She stood up with a sigh. "I'll get some paper towels, but you have to help me clean up."

"Sorry, Jill," Michael apologized. "We can get the paper towels."

"We didn't mean it," added Mark.

The two boys raced into the kitchen. A moment later they came running back in. Their dad helped them mop up the mess.

"Okay, now," Mr. Wong said. "Aren't we supposed to write our family letter to Santa tonight?"

"Oh, yes, you're right!" Mrs. Wong exclaimed. The

younger kids helped their mother clear the table and took the plates and glasses into the kitchen.

Jill hurried to the desk in the corner and took out writing paper. When everyone was sitting quietly again, Mrs. Wong began to write. " 'Dear Santa,' " she said out loud.

Jill grinned at Henry. She loved this tradition more than any other. Ever since she could remember, she had written a letter to Santa. And as she had gotten older she'd played along so that the younger children could have fun.

"Write my question first," Kristi demanded. "What do your reindeer do the rest of the year?"

Mrs. Wong wrote it down. "Okay. And I know Daddy's question—what is Mrs. Claus's favorite cookie recipe? Now, I think it's time for the wish list. Michael and Mark, tell Santa what you want most for Christmas."

The twins looked at each other. "A baby dinosaur!" they said together.

Jill laughed louder than anyone. Mrs. Wong shook her head. "It might be hard to take care of a baby dinosaur," she said. "But maybe they come with instructions. Next? Randi?"

Randi looked at her parents shyly and screwed up her face. "Do you think it would be okay if I asked for a puppy? I promise I'll take care of him. Just a little one, with a patch over one eye and white socks?"

"Have you seen a puppy like that recently, Randi?" Mr. Wong asked.

Randi nodded. "I did. Susie's dog had puppies just like that last week!"

Mr. and Mrs. Wong glanced at each other. "I see Santa is going to deliver a zoo to the Wong house." Mrs. Wong wrote down Randi's wish. "Kristi, what'll it be for you this year?"

"A telescope," Kristi said firmly. "I want to learn about the night sky and stars and stuff."

"Seems we're going to have an astronomer in the family," Mr. Wong said, nodding in approval.

"And Henry?" Mrs. Wong asked.

"Well, maybe Santa wouldn't mind bringing me some bongo drums," Henry answered. "Nice loud ones."

"Well, then, I'd like some earplugs," Jill joked, and everyone laughed.

Mr. Wong turned to his wife. "What did we ever do to have such great kids?"

"Just lucky, I guess," Mrs. Wong said, beaming. She gave him a hug.

Jill couldn't agree more. She knew she was really lucky to have such a great family.

"Okay, kids," Mrs. Wong announced, "time for bed." She and Mr. Wong started to help the younger kids upstairs.

Jill was about to get started on her homework when the telephone rang. Her mom picked it up.

"Jill," she said, smiling, "Ryan's on the phone."

Ryan! Jill jumped up eagerly. She still found it amazing that Ryan was her boyfriend. He was just so cute—

tall and athletic-looking, with long brown hair and gorgeous dark eyes. Ryan had just turned sixteen, two years older than Jill. He was fun to be with and easy to talk to. But what Jill liked most of all was the way he really seemed to care about other people.

"Hi, Ryan," Jill said when she picked up the phone.

"Hi," he answered warmly. "I hope I'm not calling too late. But I have a surprise!"

"What is it?"

"My mom said I could borrow her car. I'll have it all Sunday afternoon. I thought we could take a long drive somewhere. Into the country, maybe."

"Oh, I'd really love to, Ryan, but I can't. I have a practice session on Sunday."

"But that's your day off," Ryan protested.

"Yes, usually," Jill agreed. "But something's come up. Oh, Ryan, it's so exciting! There's going to be a huge ice show on television! It's called *Nutcracker on Ice*. They're holding auditions for it soon, and everyone in Silver Blades can try out!"

"You mean you might be on TV?" Ryan sounded impressed. "Awesome."

"I know," Jill said. "But it means extra practice sessions for a while."

Ryan was silent. "When will you try out?"

"I don't know exactly. We just heard about it today," Jill explained. "We'll find out more at tomorrow's practice. And get this—the stars are Trisha McCoy and Christopher Kane!"

"Wow. Even I've heard of them," Ryan said.

"Sure—they're two of the top skaters in the country," Jill told him.

"And they're coming here to Seneca Hills for this TV thing?" Ryan asked.

"Not exactly," Jill answered. "Some scouts are coming here for the Silver Blades auditions. But the show's going to be taped in Boston, a few days before Christmas," she explained. "Oh, Ryan, I really hope I get picked! Then my old coach, Ludmila, will see me skating on TV. And then she'll really want me back at the Ice Academy."

"Hang on," Ryan said. "When did you say the show was?"

"Just before Christmas."

Ryan sighed.

"I know," Jill said quickly, "that's the only bad part. I hate to miss any vacation here in Seneca Hills." She paused, then burst out again in excitement. "But it would definitely be worth it! National television! Isn't it exciting?"

"Yeah, I guess so," Ryan said. "But . . ."

"But what?" Jill felt uneasy. "I'll be around until then. If I even go," she added. "I mean, you do want me to go, don't you?"

"Sure. It sounds like a great opportunity," Ryan said. But he didn't sound too excited about it.

"Well, you'll keep your fingers crossed for me, right?" Jill tried to keep any worry out of her voice.

"You bet. Well, I should hang up now—" Ryan began.

"Wait," Jill cried. "Listen, I'm sorry about Sunday.

But maybe we could do something else this weekend?"

"What else? You have Saturday practice, too," Ryan said.

Jill thought for a moment. "I know—why don't you come by the rink tomorrow? We could have lunch at the snack bar."

"Okay," Ryan agreed. "Maybe I'll come early and watch you skate. Is that all right?"

"That'd be great!" said Jill happily.

"I'll see you at the rink, then. Bye."

"See you there," Jill answered brightly. But as she hung up the phone she couldn't help feeling worried. She hadn't liked the sound of Ryan's voice.

Jill finished her homework. Then she went upstairs to get ready for bed. But as she pulled on her pajamas and climbed into bed, sleep was the furthest thing from her mind. All she could think about was Ryan.

Ryan knew how much skating meant to Jill. He knew she had to put in long hours of practice every week. He said it didn't bother him. But she had heard the disappointment in his voice just now—first when she couldn't see him on Sunday, and then when she told him she might be away at Christmas.

Jill picked up Randi's old bear, Mr. Grizzly, from the end of the bed. She hugged him tightly. Before she knew it, she had stopped worrying about Ryan. Her thoughts wandered to *The Nutcracker*. It would be so great to play Clara, she thought as her eyes closed. Clara—the starring role. Her way back to the Academy. Her dream come true . . .

3

The locker room was crowded before Saturday practice. Nikki, Tori, and Haley were already there when Jill arrived. Jill called out greetings to all of them. Then she swung her plaid skate bag onto a bench and peeled off her light-blue warm-up jacket.

Jill hung her jacket in her locker and started to change. Carefully she unfolded a pair of black velvet leggings and a matching red and black striped velour top. It was one of her favorite outfits. She had chosen it with special care that morning. She really wanted to look her best for Ryan.

Jill glanced over at Tori as she started to braid her hair. Tori was changing, too. She was just zipping up a turquoise velvet skating dress. The dress had white lace trim at the collar and cuffs. Tori always had the most beautiful outfits. That was because Mrs. Carsen,

Tori's mom, was a designer. She made all Tori's skating clothes herself.

Sometimes Jill envied Tori's beautiful outfits. But Jill did *not* envy the way Tori's mom acted during practice. Mrs. Carsen used to be a competitive skater herself, and she was very critical. She didn't mind telling Tori exactly what she thought of each and every move. And her raspy voice carried far across the rink, so everyone heard what Mrs. Carsen had to say. Sometimes Jill felt really embarrassed for Tori.

Jill retied the red ribbon on her braid. "Tori, you look great today," she said.

"Thanks, Jill," Tori said matter-of-factly. "I love the way this color brings out my eyes."

Jill glanced over at Nikki. Nikki raised her eyebrows. Typical Tori, her look seemed to say.

"You look pretty great yourself, Jill," Nikki said. She ran a brush through her long brown hair. "I've always liked that top on you."

Jill smiled at the compliment and blushed slightly. "Ryan's coming to watch me practice. We're having lunch together," she said.

"Oh, really? A lunch date, huh?" Haley piped up. As usual, Haley was dressed casually. That day she wore a white T-shirt and black leggings. Her skeleton earring caught the light as she bent to finish lacing her skates. "Ryan's great," Haley said. "You're so lucky."

"Thanks," said Jill. Ryan *was* great. She was really looking forward to seeing him.

Martina walked into the locker room as Jill and Haley were talking. "Speaking of *boyfriends*," Martina said in a teasing tone, "I read the new issue of *Skating Magazine* last night. It had a fantastic story about Trisha McCoy and Christopher Kane. Isn't it romantic, the way they both skate and are in love off the ice and everything?" Martina sighed as she began to change into her skates.

"Christopher Kane is really good-looking," Tori agreed. "She's so lucky to have him as her partner."

"I think it might be the other way around," Haley said. "Trisha McCoy is unbelievably talented, if you ask me."

"I just can't believe we might skate in the same show with them," Jill added. "Just think about it—two of the top skaters in the country, in the world even, and us!"

"I wonder who the scouts are," Martina remarked.

"Do you think we might all get chosen?" Haley looked hopeful.

"Even if we do, there's only one Clara," Tori commented. "She's really the star of the show. The story is all about her. I really hope I get the part."

Jill rolled her eyes. Every girl in Silver Blades hoped to play the role of Clara, but only Tori would come out and say so, Jill thought.

"Of course, Tori," Nikki said. "We all feel the same way. But remember, the scouts are going to be looking at other skating clubs, too. We may think that Silver Blades is the best, but there are other good skaters around."

"Carla Benson, for instance," Haley added mischievously.

Carla was a talented member of the Blade Runners skating club. Everyone in Silver Blades knew about Tori's rivalry with Carla. Jill tried not to giggle, but Tori looked mad.

"Haley!" Tori exclaimed. "How could you say that to me? You know I can't stand Carla Benson!"

Haley put her arm around Tori's shoulders. "Just kidding."

"All right, I see your point," Tori admitted. "Maybe I did get carried away. But I would be terrific as Clara."

"There are other good roles, you know," Martina pointed out. "Like some of the featured roles in the second act, when Clara and the prince go to the Land of Sweets. Besides, it would be wonderful to be in the show at all."

"Martina's right," Haley agreed. "I'd love to be in the big party scene in act one. I always loved that giant Christmas tree. Wouldn't it be fun to skate a pairs program right under it? Patrick and I have already started learning the new routine." Haley's partner was Patrick McGuire. He was a sophomore in high school. With his red hair and brown eyes, he was a great match for Haley.

"You already started the routine?" Jill asked in surprise.

"Yesterday," Haley said. "And I bet you learn the singles program today."

"Then I'd better get out there and see what Kathy has for me," Jill said. "See you all on the ice!"

But when Jill got on the ice a few moments later, Kathy wasn't there. That's funny, Jill thought. Kathy is always early. She's never late.

Jill noticed Blake Michaels skating in the center of the rink. Blake was a former ice dancer. Now he worked as a choreographer, designing new programs for Silver Blades members.

"Excuse me, Blake," said Jill, skating over to him. "Have you seen Kathy? I'm supposed to have a session with her."

Blake glanced around. "She was here a few minutes ago," he commented. "I just finished showing her the new Clara routine. You'll all have to skate it for the *Nutcracker* auditions."

"Great! I can't wait to learn it," Jill said. She felt a burst of excitement. "What's it like? Is it hard?"

"It's elegant and graceful," Blake told her. "Really a beautiful piece of choreography. And not too complicated. You should have no problems with it, Jill. Oh, there's Kathy, over there, on the side."

Kathy was standing by the boards—with the young girl from the day before. The girl's mother was also with them, and Kathy was listening closely to what the woman was saying.

Jill watched them as she warmed up, feeling more and more curious. She just had to know who the girl was.

Kathy finished talking and skated over to Jill. "Hey, Jill. How are you today?" the coach asked as usual.

"Great," Jill answered. "I'm really excited about the *Nutcracker* auditions."

"I'll bet you are. I'll show you the program for Clara right now," Kathy said. "Are you warmed up enough to begin?"

"Sure." Jill hesitated. "Kathy," she asked a little shyly, "can I ask you a question first? Who is that girl you were talking to? She was here yesterday, watching me practice."

"You mean Amber," Kathy said. "Amber Armstrong. She's eleven years old, and she's here with her mother to check out the club. They came all the way from New Mexico."

Jill's eyes widened. "That's a long trip."

"It sure is," said Kathy. "But Amber's a very talented skater."

Jill knew it cost a lot of money to fly from New Mexico to Pennsylvania. She couldn't help wondering if Amber's family was rich. Skating was expensive for anyone. Because Jill had six younger brothers and sisters, money for her skating didn't come easy. Her parents often worked overtime at their jobs to earn extra money for Jill's skate time. Her father worked in a bank, helping customers with loan applications. Mrs. Wong worked in a travel agency.

Jill often wished it were easier for her parents. She tried to help them as much as she could by baby-sitting her younger siblings. Still, she sometimes dreamed of coming from a family where money was no problem.

"Jill?" Kathy interrupted her thoughts. "Let's get to work on Clara. Are you ready?"

"Absolutely," Jill replied.

As Jill glided to the center of the ice, all thoughts of Amber left her mind. She focused all her attention on the new routine Kathy was demonstrating. The moves were elegant and impressive, just as Blake had said. And not too hard at all.

Jill felt her excitement return. Ice Academy, she told herself, here comes Jill Wong!

4

Jill knew the story of *The Nutcracker* so well that it was easy to think of herself as Clara. As Jill practiced the new Clara routine she imagined she was skating with Christopher Kane. She could really feel Clara's mood, and she tried to express it in her skating. She was definitely having fun. And she always skated her best when she was enjoying herself.

The audition scene was taken from early in the story, when Clara is given the nutcracker by her mysterious godfather. Clara jumps for joy, enchanted by the funny little toy. The scene had several more jumps and then a quiet moment of happiness ending in an elegant lay-back. It was a wonderful program.

Jill knew that every singles skater in Silver Blades was planning to try out for the role. They would all learn the program. But she could see that Martina was already having a hard time with the first jump, a triple toe loop.

As if she had heard Jill's thought, Martina made the triple into a double and then landed the jump badly. Martina steadied herself and glanced over at Jill. Jill gave her a nod of encouragement. Martina shrugged and prepared to try the jump again.

Jill also began to run through the program a second time. Just then Ryan came in. He found a seat in the first row of the bleachers, near the boards. She waved, and Ryan waved back. Jill smiled to herself and decided to put in a little extra effort just for him. She was really happy to see him, and he seemed happy to see her, too.

As she glided over to her start position, Ryan gave her a huge smile and a thumbs-up sign. Jill's heart leaped a tiny bit. Each time she saw Ryan she was a little surprised by how handsome he was. Jill loved the way his brown hair curled slightly at his shoulders and the way his smile crinkled the corners of his eyes.

Jill landed her double axel perfectly and went smoothly into a flying camel. As she powered around the rink in a series of extra-strong backward crossovers, she saw Ryan watching her closely. He couldn't seem to take his eyes off her.

One more turn around the rink gave her enough speed and power to lift gracefully into the double Lutz–double loop jump combination. She felt as though she were floating above the ice. As the program slowly wound down to the final layback, Jill brought her arms gracefully above her head and came to a stop.

Jill felt really good about how she had done. She paused for a moment, then skated over to Kathy. She knew that she had skated beautifully for the first time since breaking her foot. She felt a warm glow all over, and she could see from the look on Kathy's face that her coach was impressed.

"Jill, that was a fantastic start," Kathy praised her. "Keep it up. If you polish what you've begun today, I think you have a real shot at *The Nutcracker*."

Jill did a quick spin right where she stood. "Oh, Kathy, thank you," she said. "I love this routine. And I love the music, too. I can't wait to audition for Clara."

"There are other good roles besides Clara," Kathy reminded her. "Having all the singles girls learn Clara makes it easier to judge the auditions. But you should keep an open mind. You might end up skating another role—if you get any role at all."

"I know, I know," said Jill, brushing her leggings off a bit. "But after today I really feel as if I *am* Clara."

"All right, Clara," Kathy said with a laugh. "Lunchtime. Take a break and we'll work more this afternoon."

Jill smiled and hummed a few bars of the music as she glided over to where Ryan stood waiting for her.

Standing next to him, Jill noticed again how tall Ryan was. Even with her skates on, he was taller than she was. As she slipped on her skate guards she looked up at him. His eyes were shining with admiration. He offered her his hand as she stepped off the ice.

"Jill, you were wonderful," he said.

"Thanks." She felt a burst of happiness.

"You deserve a great lunch after that workout," he said.

"Sounds good to me," Jill replied. "And I can tell you more about the ice show. You just saw the audition routine for Clara."

"The one for Boston?"

Jill glanced at him. Was Ryan's voice suddenly cold? Or was it just her imagination?

She put the question out of her mind. After all, this was one of the best days ever for her. Her skating was going well, her coach was proud of her, and her handsome boyfriend was taking her to lunch.

On their way past the rink to the snack bar, Jill noticed Mr. Weiler sitting on one of the benches. Jill knew that was unusual. Normally he worked with his students on the ice. But even though Martina still wasn't landing her triple toe loop correctly, Mr. Weiler was coaching her from the sidelines.

Mr. Weiler doesn't look very well, either, Jill thought. He must still be having stomach trouble. The coach noticed her watching him and waved. Jill waved back. She liked Mr. Weiler a lot.

Jill and Ryan passed another poster announcing the auditions for *Nutcracker on Ice*. Ryan paused to read it.

"I guess you really will have to practice extra hours to get ready for this," he said. "Are you nervous?"

"Definitely," Jill admitted. "Just thinking about being on national TV makes me nervous. That is, *if* I get a part. I hope I do, though. It would be the best Christmas present ever."

"Yeah, I guess it would." Ryan turned away, hiding his expression from Jill.

Something was wrong, Jill was sure of it.

"Come on," she said, trying to sound cheerful, "let's go get something to eat. I'm starving."

Jill led Ryan into the snack bar. She waved to Patrick McGuire. Patrick worked at the snack bar in his spare time to make extra money for his skating lessons. Jill admired his dedication. Every time she saw him she thought about how hard it must be to fit in school, practice, and work.

"That's Patrick," she told Ryan, "Haley's skating partner. I'll introduce you."

They made their way around some tables to the counter.

"Hi, Patrick," Jill greeted him. "Meet my friend Ryan. Ryan, this is Patrick."

Jill noticed that a few Silver Blades members were looking over at them with interest. She couldn't help being pleased at the attention. Jill turned back to the two boys.

"I've seen you at the high school," Patrick was saying to Ryan in a friendly tone. "Didn't you just move to Seneca Hills?"

"A while ago," Ryan said. "I already feel like I belong here."

Jill smiled.

Patrick grinned at the two of them. "Well, guess I'll see you around."

"Yeah," Ryan responded. He turned to Jill. "What do you say we order some food?"

"Sounds good to me," said Jill. "What's the special of the day?" she asked Patrick.

"Ginger and broccoli chicken stir-fry," he answered.

"Great, I'll have that and a large carrot-orange juice, please," she said. "How about you, Ryan?"

"Since I'm not in training, I'll take a cheeseburger and a large Coke," Ryan told Patrick.

"Coming right up," Patrick replied. "I'll be over with your food. Just take a seat."

Ryan and Jill found a table near the plate-glass window facing the rink. They could see the other skaters practicing, and Jill pointed out a few people.

"See, that's Tori in the turquoise, and Martina is over there, working on her triple toe loop. That's the first jump in the Clara audition program," Jill explained. "She's having a hard time with that jump. I know it took me a long time to land it."

"I guess it's pretty important for the audition, then," Ryan said.

"It is," agreed Jill. "I'm lucky I already have it down. It helps my chances of getting picked."

"Great," Ryan said. But he didn't look as though it was great. In fact, he fixed his eyes on the table.

Before Jill could say anything else, Patrick came over
with their lunch. As they began to eat, Jill searched her
mind for something to say. She couldn't think of anything. She had always felt so relaxed around Ryan
before. But right now she felt awkward and uncomfortable.

"Who's that?" Ryan suddenly asked.

Jill followed his gaze. "Her name is Amber Armstrong."

Amber had skated to the center of the rink. She began to perform an impressive program. As Jill watched,
a cold feeling settled in her stomach. Amber was amazing. She practically flew over the ice. Her jumps were
as light as a feather and very precise. Every move she
made was graceful. And every jump and spin seemed
completely easy.

"She's good," Ryan said.

Jill tried not to feel jealous, but she couldn't help it.
Amber was really, really talented. Part of her began to
hope that Amber wasn't interested in Silver Blades at
all.

For a few minutes neither Ryan or Jill said anything.
But as they watched Amber skate, Jill began to feel less
jealous and more annoyed. Amber was attracting a
crowd. There was loud applause as she landed a flaw-
less triple toe loop. Jill had only landed hers for the
first time the year before, at the age of thirteen. And
Amber had it down perfectly at eleven.

She's showing off, Jill thought to herself. I would

never skate just to get attention. A *real* skater doesn't do that. Instantly she felt ashamed of herself.

"She's incredible," Ryan exclaimed. "How old is she, anyway?"

Jill pushed the food around on her plate. "My coach said that she's eleven."

"Pretty good for just eleven," Ryan commented.

"Yes," Jill admitted. "She's definitely good."

"I guess she's in the running for *The Nutcracker*, too," Ryan said, his eyes still glued to Amber.

"I doubt it," Jill said.

"How come?" Ryan looked at Jill for the first time since Amber had begun skating.

"Well, first of all, she's not even *in* Silver Blades," Jill pointed out. "The audition is only for members."

"She could join the club," Ryan suggested.

"It's not that easy." Jill sighed and cleared her throat, trying to show Ryan that she wasn't really interested in the subject of Amber.

"She looks ready to join to me," Ryan said. "I'll bet she practices a lot, too. But then, it's easier for her."

"Easier?" Jill looked at Ryan in surprise. "What do you mean?"

"Well, she has no conflicts," Ryan said. "I mean, she doesn't have as much going on as somebody older. Like you, I mean. She doesn't have to find time for a boyfriend or anything." He shrugged. "It's just easier when you're that young."

Jill looked at Ryan in shock. What was he trying to

say? That it was too hard to have a girlfriend who was a skater? Was Ryan sorry he'd picked Jill—a skater who turned down dates because she was busy practicing?

She pushed her plate away. She couldn't eat a thing now. Their big lunch date wasn't turning out the way she had expected. For a few minutes she'd been on top of the world. But now . . .

Jill felt a pang in the bottom of her stomach. She forgot about *The Nutcracker*. She forgot about Amber. All she could think of was one thing:

What if Ryan doesn't like me anymore?

5

Amber finished her routine and skated over to the boards. Jill stood up abruptly.

"It's almost time for me to practice again," she told Ryan. "Do you want to take a walk or something?"

"Yeah, let's get some fresh air," Ryan agreed.

They left the snack bar. Jill was relieved they were getting away from Amber and the rink. Maybe Ryan would start acting like his old self again.

"Wait here," she told him. "I'll just be a second. I have to change out of my skates." Jill raced into the locker room, tore off her skates, and pulled on sneakers. She threw her skates in her locker and grabbed her parka and gloves.

When she came out of the locker room, Ryan was by the entrance, waiting for her. He was wearing his big plaid wool jacket, and he had wrapped a forest-green scarf around his neck.

He's so cute, Jill thought. I don't want to lose him.

Ryan held the swinging doors for her. Outside, they each took a deep breath of fresh air. Fresh-fallen snow covered the ground, and a few kids were having a snowball fight.

"Let's walk down this pathway under the trees," Jill suggested. "I just love how the snow makes everything look so pretty."

"Me too," Ryan agreed.

Jill began to feel better.

"So, what's *The Nutcracker* about, anyway?" Ryan asked as they walked along.

"You never read it when you were little?" Jill asked in surprise.

"Well, I guess so, but that was a long time ago," Ryan replied. "All I remember is a sword fight between some guy and a mouse with lots of heads. Is that the same story?"

"That's *part* of the story," Jill said with a laugh. "The nutcracker is really a prince. He fights the Mouse King, who has seven heads. And then the prince takes Clara off to the Land of Sweets. They meet people from different countries there, even fairies. That part is so beautiful. Like the Sugarplum Fairy, the role Trisha McCoy is going to skate."

"Right." Ryan nodded. "Sounds like a great show," he said, but Jill could tell he didn't mean it. Ryan gazed around silently for a moment and then turned back to Jill. "It's probably time for you to go back, right?"

Jill felt a burst of dismay. Was Ryan glad to get rid of her? "I have a couple more minutes," she said.

"Yeah, but I should get going," Ryan told her.

"Okay," Jill said. After all, she reminded herself, she did have to practice. She didn't want to just dream about getting the role of Clara.

They walked back to the rink, not saying much. At the doors of the rink they stopped to say good-bye. Ryan leaned over and gave her a quick kiss on the cheek. Before Jill could say anything, he jammed his hands in his pockets and hurried off.

Jill stared after him. Did Ryan still like her, or not? Feeling upset and confused, Jill headed back into the locker room. As she sat down to put on her skates, someone else came in. She looked up.

Oh, great, she thought.

"Hi," the girl said. "My name is Amber."

"Uh, hello," Jill said, a little stiffly. "I'm Jill Wong."

"I know," Amber said simply. To Jill's surprise, Amber sat down right next to her. "I've been watching you skate."

"I noticed." Jill got up to brush and rebraid her hair, avoiding Amber's eyes in the mirror. Why did she have to sit right next to me? she thought. I want to be alone right now.

Amber opened her skate bag and pulled out a sandwich.

That's odd, Jill thought. Why doesn't she just get something at the snack bar like all the other skaters?

Amber saw Jill watching her and she blushed a little bit. "Oh, um, I-I don't eat fast food," Amber explained, stammering a little. "It's too junky. I really watch my nutrition." Then she looked down at the floor.

"Oh. That's, uh, nice," Jill muttered.

"Kathy coaches you, right?" Amber asked.

"Yes, she does," Jill answered.

"I've had a couple of private sessions with her. She seems really nice. Maybe a little too easygoing, even," Amber commented.

"Easygoing? Sarge?" Jill asked in amazement. Amber didn't know what she was talking about. Jill looked directly at the younger girl. "Kathy's a great coach," she said. "She's probably just trying to make you feel comfortable. She placed fourth in the Nationals, you know."

"She told me," Amber said, nodding. "Why didn't she place higher?"

Jill stared at the other girl in surprise. "I never asked her." Did Amber actually expect Jill to ask Kathy something like that? "Why don't you ask her yourself?" she suggested.

"Maybe I will," Amber said calmly. She took another bite of her sandwich. "I saw Blake Michaels show Kathy the Clara routine. It seems pretty nice, don't you think?"

Jill nodded silently. Of course it's a nice routine, she

thought. It was for a nationally televised ice show . . . a show that Jill planned to be in.

"What about the other coach, Mr. Weiler?" Amber went on. "He has a funny accent. Where's he from, anyway?"

"Mr. Weiler is from Germany," Jill answered slowly. "He won a silver medal in the Olympics during the sixties." Boy, Amber sure asks a lot of questions, Jill thought. Is she this nosy about *everybody*?

"Who's the blond girl in the turquoise dress, the one who's so pretty?" Amber didn't seem to notice Jill's growing impatience.

"That's Tori Carsen." Jill finished with her hair and stuffed her brush into her bag. "She placed third at the Regionals at Lake Placid last year."

"What about the girl who can't land her triple toe loop?" Amber went on, to Jill's amazement. "I landed my triple toe loop six months ago," Amber told her. "How about you?"

"I landed it on a regular basis about a year ago," Jill said, annoyed. "And for your information," she added, "that was my friend Martina who missed the triple toe loop." Jill narrowed her eyes at Amber. "She joined Silver Blades only a year ago. So don't count her out on the toe loop. She's very dedicated."

"She'll need to be," Amber said matter-of-factly.

Jill couldn't believe it. Here was Amber, not even a member of Silver Blades, acting as though she were the best skater in the rink and trying to outrank everyone.

Amber chewed slowly on her sandwich and leaned against the mirror. "Do you always wear red?" she asked, not noticing how angry Jill was becoming. "I think it looks good on you."

Jill pretended not to hear. She glanced at the clock. It was time for her to meet Kathy again.

"I'm ranked first at our rink in New Mexico," Amber offered.

Jill rolled her eyes and closed her locker with a slam. "I'd love to hear all about it, but it's time for my afternoon session." Jill turned on her heel and left.

"Bye-bye," Amber called after her.

Jill was walking so fast that she practically collided with Tori and Mrs. Carsen on their way into the locker room.

"Oh, I'm really sorry," Jill apologized to Mrs. Carsen. "I wasn't looking where I was going."

"Jill," Tori asked, "is something wrong? You look upset."

"It's that new girl," Jill said, lowering her voice. "Amber Armstrong. She's so pushy. It just gets on my nerves."

"Believe me, Jill," Mrs. Carsen sympathized in her distinctive raspy voice, "we know exactly what you mean. She's awful. I thought her little display this morning was very showy."

Jill felt encouraged by Mrs. Carsen's comment. "It's not that I want to talk behind anybody's back," Jill said, "but you should have heard her grilling me in the locker room just now."

Tori raised her eyebrows dramatically. "Really?" she said.

"Well, yes." Jill hesitated. Should she talk about Amber like this? she wondered. But then Jill remembered how nosy Amber was. If she doesn't want people to talk about her, she shouldn't talk about them, Jill reassured herself.

"She asked me about you, Tori, and about Kathy, Mr. Weiler, and Martina. And then she started on me," Jill blurted out. "When did I start landing the triple toe loop, and do I always wear red? Then she bragged that she's ranked first at her rink in New Mexico."

Tori and her mother exchanged glances and raised eyebrows, and Jill had to smile. Even though Tori's mom could be overbearing, the Carsens were obviously very close.

"What did she want to know about me?" Tori asked eagerly.

"Just who you were and stuff," Jill answered. "I said that you placed at Lake Placid."

"Well, Jill, we'll see you soon," Mrs. Carsen said as she pushed Tori toward the locker room. "By the way, I thought you skated beautifully this morning."

"Thank you, Mrs. Carsen," Jill said.

"See you later, Jill," Tori called.

"Bye." Jill gazed after Tori and her mother. Talking to the Carsens had definitely made her feel better. Now she felt as if she had someone on her side. And at least she wasn't the only one who had noticed how annoying Amber was.

6

Later that afternoon, Jill caught up with Nikki, Martina, and Tori in front of the Seneca Hills mall.

"Hi, guys," she said. "Where's Dani? She said she'd be here. And she was supposed to pick up Haley, too."

"You know Dani's always late," Tori said.

Just then Mrs. Panati, Danielle's grandmother, pulled up in her Volvo. Haley and Danielle jumped out and waved to the other girls.

"We're here! Sorry we're late," Danielle exclaimed. She leaned into the car and kissed her grandmother. Danielle's soft brown hair curled over the shoulders of her jean jacket. She was wearing a black turtleneck over a plaid skirt with black tights.

Jill walked up to the car. "Hi, Mrs. Panati," she greeted the gray-haired woman.

Mrs. Panati gave her a big smile. "Jill, so nice to see you. It's been too long."

Back when Danielle was a member of Silver Blades, her grandmother had sometimes given Jill a ride to the rink. Now that Danielle had quit skating and joined the school newspaper, Jill hardly ever saw Mrs. Panati.

"How's your family, Jill?" Mrs. Panati asked. "Good?"

"Great," Jill answered.

"You girls have fun today. Enjoy your afternoon off. Dani, don't forget to call me when you're ready to leave," Mrs. Panati added. With a wave she drove off.

The six girls turned to go into the mall. Throughout the large central hall, big red ribbons and pine branches covered with artificial snow decorated the balconies. Gold stars and giant snowflakes hung from the ceiling, and Christmas scenes filled the center. Scattered here and there were little statues of woodland animals. Some of them were posed as if they were having snowball fights. Others were wrapping presents, and another group was arranged around a big statue of Santa by a giant fir tree.

"Doesn't it look great?" Jill unbuttoned her burgundy corduroy jacket, which she wore over black jeans.

"Definitely," Tori agreed.

"I love your outfit, Tori," Jill commented, noting Tori's matching green and white striped skirt and top.

"Oh, thanks. It's new," Tori replied. "My mom got it from Arnold's."

Tori's mother was divorced. Her new boyfriend was

Roger Arnold, of Arnold's department stores. Mrs. Carsen's clothing designs were featured there, and Tori shopped for new outfits at Arnold's all the time.

Martina, Nikki, and Haley walked ahead. Jill strolled along with Tori and Danielle.

"I'm so excited about the auditions for the ice show. Haley told me all about it. I wish I could be there!" Danielle exclaimed. "I wonder if there's a story in it? The editor of the school paper might like an insider's view of the auditions and everything. If I could get the assignment, I could tag along with you guys."

"That would be great," Jill replied.

"I'll ask the editor tomorrow," Danielle decided.

The three girls caught up with Nikki, Haley, and Martina, who were looking at cowboy boots in the window of Buckaroos, the western wear store.

"Aren't those the greatest?" Nikki sighed. She pointed at a shiny pair of black boots with red stitching up the sides and playing cards in white and red leather across the top. "They'd be perfect with my black skirt and the red and white checked top."

"You'd better tell Santa," Jill joked.

"I guess so. Those are probably pretty expensive," said Nikki.

"Probably," Martina added. "And it's bad enough having to buy new skates all the time."

The girls continued window-shopping. They stopped in front of Canady's, a popular clothing store.

"Look at those jackets," Tori said admiringly. She pointed at some cropped wool jackets that flared out at the waist. They were all the same style, but came in four bright colors: aqua, hot pink, purple, and yellow. "Those would almost make good skating outfits," she said.

"That one would match your new skating skirt, Martina," Jill said, pointing to the aqua-colored jacket.

"It would be perfect," Martina agreed. "I'd better write Santa, too," she said with a laugh.

"Speaking of perfect outfits," said Tori, "I saw another article about Trisha McCoy and Christopher Kane. This one was in *Sports World* magazine. They had this great picture of them, and Trisha had on the most beautiful dress—pink chiffon and satin. She looked like a princess. I'm going to ask my mom if she can design me something like that for the *Nutcracker* auditions."

"Tori, you're so lucky that your mother can sew," Nikki replied. "Even if my mom could, she's way too busy with the baby to do anything like that."

Nikki had a new baby brother at home named Benjamin. It was amazing to Nikki how such a little person could take up so much of a family's time.

"Just remember, girls," Haley interrupted in a serious tone, "new outfits may be nice, but it's still the skating that counts."

"Haley's right," Jill agreed. "We're each going to have to do our best on that audition program."

"Jill skated the program really well yesterday," Tori told Danielle. "She probably didn't tell you. She's so modest."

"Unlike someone else we know," Haley said slyly.

"Haley!" Tori started chasing Haley down the mall. Jill laughed out loud. It was amazing the way Haley teased Tori. No one else even dared. Tori chased Haley back to where Jill was standing.

"Hey, Tori, did that article say anything about Trisha McCoy and Christopher Kane having another of their famous fights?" Martina asked.

"My parents had a big fight last night, but it didn't make the papers," Haley said, forcing a little laugh.

"Seriously," Martina continued, "it seems like Kane and McCoy are constantly fighting and making up."

"I was being serious, too," Haley said quietly.

Jill stopped walking. "Haley, do you want to talk about it?" She looked at Haley. But her friend avoided her gaze.

"No, not really," Haley answered. "I shouldn't have said anything." She shrugged. "It was just a fight."

Tori put her arm around Haley's shoulders.

"Cheer up," she said. "It's Christmas and you're gonna have a good time," she added in a playful voice. "Or else!"

The girls all laughed. Tori could be really funny and sweet sometimes. Jill was grateful to have such good friends. She squeezed Haley's arm, and Haley looked happy again.

They came to a new store called Do Right! Its windows were crammed with hair accessories—barrettes, headbands, ribbons, and ponytail holders. Jill stood still and gazed with longing at the dazzling display. She needed to keep her long hair away from her face while she skated, and she always had an eye out for new hair bows or barrettes or scrunchies.

"Hey, let's stop in here for a minute," Jill suggested, one foot already in the door.

"This is really nice." Tori looked around the store, nodding in approval.

"Jill," Nikki called. "Look at this headband. It's perfect for you!" She held up a red velvet headband trimmed with ribbon and a bow. The ribbon was laced with gold thread.

"Oh, I love it!" Jill exclaimed. "Let me try it on."

She slipped on the headband and peered closely in a mirror on the glass counter.

"Wow, that looks great," commented Danielle.

Jill smiled at her reflection. She had to admit that the red and gold was beautiful against her shining black hair.

Reluctantly she took off the headband. She didn't have much money with her and she needed to buy some Christmas presents for her family. She really wanted to get Henry some bongo music for his Walkman. She'd have to come back for the headband another time.

"Do you have any more of these, or is this the only one?" Jill asked the salesperson behind the counter.

"We have some on order," she replied, "but right now that's the only one we've got."

"Well, maybe I'll be back later," Jill said, and tried the headband on again, admiring the shade of red in the mirror. She turned to Tori. "Don't you think it would be perfect for the auditions?"

"Absolutely. It's you!" Tori exclaimed.

The other girls nodded in agreement.

Jill put the headband back in the display rack, deciding to come back another time to get it. Maybe it would bring her luck during the audition.

"Hey, look!" Nikki exclaimed. "Isn't that Amber, the girl who was at the rink yesterday?"

Jill turned. Amber was watching her through the store window. She was wearing a white T-shirt and faded jeans with a blue cardigan. Jill noticed that Amber's sweater seemed a little small for her, as though it belonged to a younger sister.

Jill sighed. The last thing she needed right now was another grilling from Amber. Why did she always show up wherever Jill was? It was as if Amber was following her around.

Just then Amber's mother appeared. She joined her daughter at the window.

"Let's get away from here," Jill suggested. They all walked out of the store and across the mall, looking at a window that had pretty dresses on display.

"I heard Amber might be moving to Seneca Hills," Nikki said. "I think she's from Mexico or something."

"I heard that, too," Martina added. "But I thought it was Texas, or some place out West." She shrugged. "Anyway, she's a pretty good skater."

"I think she's sweet-looking," Nikki said.

"She's only ten, I think," said Haley. "And I heard she's going to study with Mr. Weiler."

"Actually, she's studying with Kathy," Jill said quietly. "While she's here, that is. Kathy said she's eleven and she's from *New* Mexico."

"You talked to her in the locker room, right, Jill?" Tori said. "Remember, you said she was really pushy, asking you all those questions about us and everything."

"Really?" Danielle interrupted. "What kind of questions?"

"Everything!" Jill sighed. The last thing she wanted to do was talk about Amber.

Dani nodded. "What else do you know about her?"

"Not much." Jill sighed. "She said she was top-ranked at her rink. And Kathy did say that she's very talented."

"We all know that," Tori said huffily. "You should have seen the way she was showing off on the ice yesterday."

"Why do you say that?" Danielle asked.

"Because she was doing a lot of flashy jumps just to get attention." Tori sniffed.

"I thought she was really good," Martina said. "She can't help it if people like watching her practice."

"Do you think she's going to be invited to join Silver Blades?" Danielle asked. "If she's so talented, it sounds like it would be good to have her in the club."

"I hope not," Tori said. "There's no room for a show-off."

"Oh, no?" Haley grinned.

Tori pretended to be offended. "I am not a show-off, even if I am a great skater."

"You're right." Haley laughed. "I take it back."

"Hey, maybe I should interview Amber for the paper," Danielle suggested. "It's not every day a new skater moves here. That could even be a good angle for my skating story."

Jill couldn't believe it. It was too much. *Everywhere I turn, it's Amber, Amber, Amber,* she complained to herself. *She's really getting on my nerves!*

"Enough about Amber," Jill declared. "I'm hungry and I want a frozen yogurt, *now*!"

"I'm hungry, too," Haley agreed. "Super Sundaes is definitely the next stop."

"Come on, then," Jill said.

As the group of girls passed the Do Right! hair accessories store on their way to Super Sundaes, Jill looked through the window. Amber was inside. And she was trying on the red velvet headband!

The others followed her gaze. "Hey, she's trying on your headband, Jill," Tori said with surprise.

"Red is definitely *not* her color," Jill retorted. Amber was really beginning to bug her. First she had acted as if she were the greatest skater ever to hit Seneca Hills. Then she had started taking lessons with Jill's coach. And now she was trying on the headband Jill wanted for herself. Jill shook her head. "Come on. Super Sundaes is waiting," she told her friends. She walked quickly away.

As she passed Canady's clothing store Jill stopped short. She had almost bumped right into Ryan!

"Ryan!" she exclaimed. "What are you doing here?" She flushed, feeling uncomfortable.

"Oh, Jill. Hi." Ryan looked around. He didn't seem too comfortable, either. "I, uh, I was just looking for something, that's all."

"In Canady's?" said Tori, raising her eyebrows.

"Um, yeah. I mean n-no," Ryan said, stammering a little. His face turned red.

"We're going to Super Sundaes for some ice cream. Why don't you come?" Jill invited him.

"No, thanks," Ryan answered quickly. "I mean, I can't. I have to—" He paused. "I have to do something," he finished.

"Oh," Jill said. "Well, okay, fine."

"See you later, Jill," Ryan said, and hurried off.

"He sure was in a rush," Martina commented. The other girls stared after Ryan in surprise. Jill tried not to show how upset she was.

"I guess he had something important to do," Nikki offered. She squeezed Jill's arm.

"Yeah," said Jill, feeling her lower lip begin to tremble. "Something more important to him than me."

"Oh, Jill!" Danielle threw an arm around Jill's shoulders. "Don't even think that."

"Yeah," said Haley, "everybody knows Ryan's crazy about you."

"He *used* to be crazy about me," Jill said, trying not to cry. "But he's been acting so strange lately." She drew in a shaky breath. "I think he's not interested in me anymore."

"He *was* acting awfully suspicious just now," Tori commented. "Coming out of a girls' clothing store and then rushing off, all secretive and everything."

"Tori!" said Haley sharply. "What are you trying to do, get Jill more upset?"

"No, of course not," Tori protested. "It's just that—" She stopped as Haley shot her a warning look.

"It's okay," said Jill in a low voice. "Tori's right. Ryan *was* acting weird." She paused. "You don't think he has another girlfriend, do you?"

"Oh, no," Haley said quickly.

"Of course not," Nikki immediately agreed. "Don't be silly."

"Well, it would sort of explain the weird way he was behaving," offered Tori. "But I'm sure it's not true," she added.

"Jill, did something happen between you?" Nikki finally asked.

Jill nodded. She was so relieved to talk about it that the words came pouring out. "He's been upset since this whole *Nutcracker* thing started! He asked me for a special date, and I couldn't go because I added a Sunday practice. And I already spend so much time skating! And then he was talking about how Amber is lucky that she's still too young to worry about finding time for boys and dates, and . . . and I just know he's not happy with me anymore!" Tears streamed down Jill's face.

Immediately Dani, Nikki, Martina, and Haley surrounded her. "Oh, Jill," Dani cried, "I know that's not true!"

"Look, Jill," said Haley. "If you're really worried about this, there's only one thing to do."

"You mean spy on him?" suggested Tori.

"No," said Haley quickly. "Talk to him about it."

"Haley's right," said Martina. "If Ryan really has been acting strange lately and you want to know why, you should just ask him, Jill."

"Yeah," agreed Nikki. "It's the only way to get to the bottom of this."

Jill thought about it. "Sure. I guess you guys are right," she said. "If there's something going on, the best thing to do is talk about it."

Martina and the others nodded in agreement. They all looked pleased, as though the whole thing was settled. But to Jill, it was anything *but* settled. She could never come right out and ask Ryan what was wrong, never in a million years. The whole idea was just too scary.

Because, Jill thought fearfully, what if I ask what's going on—and Ryan says he's found another girl?

7

At Monday morning's practice, Jill reviewed the Clara program in her mind one more time. When she felt ready, she raised her arms to the start position. She wanted to improve the way she changed from one move to the next, especially when she went from the double Lutz–double loop combination into the layback spin. She reminded herself of Kathy's suggestion that she pace her breathing, taking deeper breaths between each jump.

Jill was so nervous about this audition. She almost wished that getting the role of Clara didn't mean so much to her. But it did. She had worked so hard to get to the Academy and been so disappointed when she had to leave. Now she was willing to work even harder to return there.

As she finished the program she glanced around the

rink. Amber was skating nearby. Across from her, Tori also skated on her own, waiting for Mr. Weiler. That's funny, Jill thought. It's the second time he's been late. The coach had always been on time before, and he expected his students to be on time, too.

Kathy interrupted her thoughts. "Okay, Jill, that was nice," her coach said. "Let's try it again. And remember about the breathing. You have to be relaxed going into the layback."

Just then Tori skated over.

"Kathy, I'm sorry to bother you," Tori began, "but do you know where Mr. Weiler is?"

"I'm afraid I don't," Kathy answered. "Why don't you try skating a little bit longer on your own? I'm sure he'll be here soon."

Mrs. Carsen came over to the boards nearest Kathy. A long pink cashmere coat was draped over her shoulders, and she wore a white silk scarf tied at her throat.

"Kathy, I don't understand what's gotten into Mr. Weiler," she complained. "He knows the auditions are coming up soon. Every minute of practice counts."

"Yes, Mrs. Carsen, you're right," Kathy replied patiently. "Which is why I suggested that Tori continue practicing as best she can until Mr. Weiler gets here." She pulled back a stray strand of hair that had escaped from her ponytail.

"Well, this is awfully frustrating," Mrs. Carsen said, her eyes searching the rink. She turned to Tori. "Okay," she barked, "you heard Kathy. Go practice. Let's see you do a layback as nice as Jill's."

Tori sighed. "Mom, take it easy," she said.

Kathy and Jill exchanged quiet smiles, and the coach shrugged. "Mrs. Carsen seems to approve of your lay-back," Kathy commented. "But I think it still needs a little work. Can you try arching your back more, like this?" Kathy demonstrated, pulling up from her torso with grace.

Jill did as Kathy asked, stretching her spine.

"Better," Kathy said encouragingly. "Don't forget to breathe, though. You're clenching when you should be relaxing. Take it again."

Jill continued to work on her layback. Glancing up, she caught Amber watching her closely. Can't she give me a break? Jill thought with annoyance. She tried to keep her focus as she spun into another layback, but she made the same mistake again, tensing up her shoulders when she should have let them stretch.

Kathy skated up to her. "Try to clear your mind, Jill. What are you thinking about?"

Jill glanced over at Amber, and Kathy followed her gaze. Jill looked down in embarrassment.

"Try not to think about anybody else's work," Kathy told her. "You're doing very well with this program."

"Thanks," Jill said.

"Now let's see you do the double axel followed by the flying camel," said Kathy. "We'll come back to the lay-back a little later."

Jill skated around the rink, reviewing the jump in her mind. She kept her arms relaxed as she kicked her right leg forward. Then she immediately brought her arms close in to her body as she sprang into the air. She completed two and half revolutions, then landed on her right outside edge. It wasn't quite perfect, but she continued into the crossovers that led to the flying camel. She swung her leg around, being sure to keep her arms out straight and her chin lifted up.

"You're overrotating your shoulders in the double axel, Jill. That's costing you some height and making those revolutions look a little sloppy," Kathy commented. "Take it again."

When Jill turned to start the combination over, she saw Amber skating nearby. Amber was doing the exact same moves Jill had just been working on. Jill had to admit that Amber made the series of jumps and spins seem effortless.

Shaken that Amber would dare imitate her, Jill's eyes began to tear up. She bent to smooth out her leggings, hiding her face so that Kathy wouldn't see how upset she was. It was as if Amber was deliberately trying to embarrass her.

With effort, Jill blinked back her tears. Then she straightened up. If Amber really wants to be competitive, I'll show her what competitive is all about, Jill thought, gritting her teeth.

She cleared her mind and focused. She felt calm inside and concentrated, certain now that she would execute the move perfectly. She powered up again, and this time when she lifted off the ice for the double axel, she used all the strength of her thighs, gaining enough height to complete the revolutions flawlessly. She landed smoothly and swept into the crossovers for the flying camel with speed and grace.

"Excellent," Kathy called. "See how well you do when you're not distracted?"

Just then Kathy was paged to the office for a phone call.

"Sorry, Jill," she apologized. "It must be important. Keep working, and I'll be right back."

Kathy glided off the ice. Jill watched her go, then turned to resume practice. At that moment Amber skated right up behind her.

"That last double axel was much better," Amber said.

"Thanks for noticing," Jill responded sarcastically.

"Are you having a hard time going from the flying camel into the next section?" Amber asked. "Isn't that a double Lutz–double loop?"

"Yes, it is, but no, I'm not having a hard time with it," Jill answered coldly.

"Well, could you tell me what Kathy said about the layback?" Amber asked, mentioning the last move in the Clara program.

Jill narrowed her eyes. Amber was really going too far, grilling her about the *Nutcracker* program. She wasn't even eligible for the *Nutcracker* tryouts, but it didn't seem to stop her.

"Excuse me, Amber, but I really have to practice," Jill said sharply. "If you want to know what Kathy thinks about the layback, ask her yourself."

She skated away, feeling as if she were going to explode. Her anger spilled over into her skating, and she jumped with so much force that she could barely land simple waltz jumps.

She couldn't get Amber out of her mind. Imagine interrupting *my* practice time to ask me questions about *my* audition program. Who does she think she is?

Just then Kathy hurried out of the office. Her face was white, and she looked worried. She motioned Jill and Tori over to the boards. Mrs. Carsen noticed and hurried after them. She pointed her sunglasses at Kathy.

"Listen, Kathy, this is absurd," she rasped. "Practice is practically over! Can't you find out where Mr. Weiler is?"

"Really," Tori whined. "I can't do *everything* on my own. I need my coach!"

Kathy took a deep breath. "I know where Mr. Weiler is. And it's bad news," she told them. "He's in the hospital!"

8

Jill and the Carsens gasped together. "The hospital?" Mrs. Carsen raised a hand to her throat. "What happened? What's wrong?"

"He had a heart attack," Kathy said quietly. "He's in Grandview Memorial Hospital and he's resting."

"A heart attack?" Tori shrieked.

"Is he okay?" Jill was beginning to feel scared.

"How serious is it, Kathy?" Mrs. Carsen asked.

Kathy laid a hand on Mrs. Carsen's arm to calm her. "It was fairly serious, but they think he'll be all right. He just needs time to recover."

Some other skaters had been attracted by Tori's loud shriek. They crowded around, and the news spread. A few of the youngest skaters looked as if they might cry. Nikki ran up to Jill with her pairs partner, Alex Beekman.

"Is Mr. Weiler okay?" Nikki asked in a whisper.

"I don't know," Jill answered, her voice tight. "Kathy said it was pretty serious."

Hilary Ford, one of Mr. Weiler's younger skaters, pulled on Jill's sleeve. Jill could see how scared she was. Her big blue eyes were filled with fear. Hilary was only nine. This must be hard for her, Jill realized, thinking of her younger brothers and sisters at home. But then, it was hard for everybody.

Jill put her arm around Hilary. "Don't worry," she said. "Mr. Weiler's in a great hospital. The doctors will take very good care of him."

Kathy raised her voice above all the talking. "Listen, everybody. Mr. Weiler is in serious condition, but the doctors said he should have a fine recovery," she announced. "I'm going over there now. I'll be back with more news as soon as I can."

Jill noticed that Amber stood apart from the group, and she looked a little pale.

"Kathy, just a minute," called Mrs. Carsen. "Who's going to coach Tori if Mr. Weiler is in the hospital?"

"I can't possibly answer that at this moment, Mrs. Carsen." Kathy's tone was exasperated. "But I promise everything will work out eventually. Right now I'd like to find out more about Mr. Weiler's condition."

"Kathy," Nikki piped up, "is there anything we can do to help?"

Kathy stopped for a moment and considered. "I'm sure Mr. Weiler would appreciate knowing you're thinking of him. Maybe you could make a card or something like that. That would be nice."

Kathy slipped away from the crowd, pulling her coat closed over her skating clothes.

Jill stood with Nikki, Alex, Tori, and Josh Buskirk, who had skated pairs with Tori in last year's Ice Spectacular. Josh pointed to an older skater, Mitchell Bowen, who was standing to one side.

"Maybe Mitchell knows something else," said Josh. "After all, his mom is the president of Silver Blades."

"Let's ask him," Jill responded. She skated over to Mitchell.

"Have you heard anything from your mom, Mitchell?" she asked.

Mitchell shook his head. "I'm not sure she knows yet," he said. "Boy, I really hope he's going to be all right."

Nikki skated up behind Jill. "Maybe we can get the card organized for this afternoon," she suggested. "It's almost time to go to school, anyway. We're not going to get more skating in after this."

"You're right, Nikki," Mitchell agreed. "Do you guys have any ideas for it?"

"Well, Dani can help," Jill replied. "She has a friend who does drawings for the paper. I know he could give us ideas. I'll bet we could have a card ready for this afternoon."

By the afternoon practice, Jill and Nikki had the card ready. Martina and Tori helped them spread it flat on one of the benches for everyone to sign. It was very long and narrow, like a banner. Danielle's friend had helped them design a border of skates and ribbons that ran along the edges. The border was printed in light blue to go with the white background.

"Blue and white," Martina said, looking pleased. "The official colors of Silver Blades."

"Dani's friend did a great job," Tori agreed.

"And he printed it on the newspaper's computer," Jill told them. She read the card out loud: " 'Get well soon, Mr. W. We miss you already! Love, Silver Blades.' "

The members of Silver Blades lined up to sign the card. Jill smiled reassuringly at Kelly O'Reilly. Kelly was only in fourth grade. She stuck the tip of her tongue out between her teeth as she drew a flower next to her name, then smiled as she gave the pen back to Jill.

"That's sweet, Kelly," Jill commented. "I'm sure Mr. Weiler will like it."

"I hope so," Kelly said. "I hope it makes him feel better."

Jill realized that Mr. Weiler was the only coach Kelly had ever worked with. It was the same for many of the younger kids. The news was hardest on them.

"I think everyone has signed," Tori said, reading the card over.

"Good," Jill responded. "Then let's give it to Kathy. She can take it to the hospital later."

"I hope he recovers soon," Martina said wistfully. "I had a hard time concentrating in school today. I just kept worrying about him."

"Me too," Nikki said. "I didn't realize how much I'd miss him."

As Jill gave Nikki a comforting squeeze Amber approached. She gave Jill a big smile.

"Hi," she said. "I didn't sign the card yet. I want to say get well to Mr. Weiler, if that's okay."

Tori snatched the card up from the bench and folded it. "Well, Amber," she said, "this *is* a card from Silver Blades. But if you want to send Mr. Weiler a get-well card on your own, I'm sure he'd appreciate it."

"Tori, it's true that Amber's not in the club. But one more signature can't hurt," Martina said.

"Besides," Nikki added, "I'm sure Mr. Weiler will appreciate every good wish he gets."

Amber put out her hand for the card. "Thanks," she told Martina and Nikki. She turned to Jill. "Can I use your pen?"

Jill hesitated, but gave the pen to Amber. Amber signed her name in huge letters—right under Jill's signature!

She gave Jill another big smile, then hurried into the locker room.

"I don't believe it," Tori exclaimed. "She has the biggest signature here. And she's not even Mr. Weiler's student!"

"And why did she have to sign right under *my* name?" Jill cried. "She really gets on my nerves." She sighed. "Oh, well. Martina is right. If it makes Mr. Weiler feel better, it's worth it."

Jill carried the card toward Kathy's office. But before

she got there, Kathy bustled out with her coat on. She was with a short, thick-set blond man. He was older than Kathy, maybe in his late thirties. Jill thought she had seen him before, but she couldn't remember where.

"Excuse me," Jill said, holding the card out, "but we've all signed this. We were hoping you could take it to Mr. Weiler today."

"Isn't this nice!" Kathy admired the card. "I know this will cheer him up. I'm leaving for the hospital right now. I can't wait to give it to him. See you later, Jill." She turned to the man beside her. "Dan, I'm sure you'll have everything under control. I'll try to be back before practice is over."

"Great, Kathy. Give my very best to Franz," he said with a warm smile.

Kathy waved good-bye.

Dan turned to Jill, holding out his hand. "You must be Jill Wong. Pleased to meet you." He shook Jill's hand firmly. "I'm Dan Trapp. Let's go talk to the rest of the gang."

Without a backward glance to see if she was following, Dan marched over to the waiting members of Silver Blades.

Dan Trapp! Jill thought. Of course. Now she knew why he looked familiar. Dan Trapp had once been a top competitor. She had read about his performance at the Worlds.

But what is Dan Trapp doing here in Seneca Hills? Jill wondered.

She hurried to catch up with him. She didn't want to miss a word of what he was going to say.

Dan stood at the boards and waved his arms in a big circle. "I'd like everyone's attention for a few minutes," he announced with a broad smile. "Don't be shy, now. Come closer, I'm not going to bite anyone. That's right."

Turning to little Hilary Ford, he gently took her hand to bring her forward in the crowd.

"Can you see now?" he asked.

Hilary giggled and nodded.

"Now, I know you're all wondering who I am," he went on. "My name is Dan Trapp." He smiled. "The Dan Trapp who placed in the Worlds about the same time that most of you were learning how to walk."

There was a murmur of surprise from the skaters. Dan waited patiently for the noise to die down.

"Now, some of you Silver Blades skaters are going to need a new coach," he said. "Well—that's me." Dan jabbed his chest with his thumb and grinned. "I'm your new coach."

There was a moment of silence. Jill felt stunned. And from the looks on everyone's faces, all the members of Silver Blades felt the same way.

New coach? Jill thought. Did that mean Mr. Weiler was never coming back?

9

⸙

"**I** know this comes as a surprise, but I'm filling in until Mr. Weiler gets back on his feet," Dan explained. "And I promise you, I am going to do my super-duper best! I'll make sure that you *all* get the top-rate coaching that a great club like Silver Blades deserves. I'm thrilled to help out. And I couldn't be more excited about taking over Mr. Weiler's students."

Jill caught Haley's eye. Haley raised her eyebrows and shrugged.

"Now, our number-one task is to make sure that these auditions for *Nutcracker on Ice* go well," he went on. "I'm here to make sure that happens. You're going to be spectacular. And we're going to do it together!" he said with enthusiasm. "Now, who has a question?"

"I don't have a question, but I *do* have something to

say," Tori announced. "*I* want to be coached by Kathy." She gave Dan a defiant look.

Jill waited to see how Dan would react to Tori's insulting tone. Would he get angry?

But it seemed to roll right off him.

"As far as Kathy's time is concerned, we're going to have to be understanding," Dan said without missing a beat. "Not only does she have her hands completely full running Silver Blades without Mr. Weiler, but her coaching time is booked solid."

"Well, then, I want Blake to coach me," Tori said stubbornly.

"Blake?" Dan looked confused. "Oh, Blake Michaels, the choreographer? But he's not a coach, you know that." Dan spoke directly to Tori. "We're going to be a great team, you'll see." He gave her a wink.

Tori was clearly unimpressed by Dan's chummy attitude. She rolled her eyes. "Oh, brother," she muttered under her breath.

Jill couldn't help glancing at Amber, who stood quietly on the edge of the crowd. Tori didn't know why Kathy's time was booked so solid. But Jill did. Amber had taken Kathy's last coaching slot.

Wait until Tori hears this one, Jill thought. And Mrs. Carsen, too. Tori's mom would definitely put up a fight when she heard that Kathy's time was being taken up by someone who wasn't even a member of Silver Blades. Jill could just imagine the scene the Carsens would make!

"Now, I hope everybody is ready to get back out on

the ice!" Dan made eye contact around the group. "Don't forget, we're here to skate. That's what Mr. Weiler would want us to do."

Hilary looked up at him, seeming uncertain.

Dan gave her a smile of encouragement. "Are you ready to skate?" he asked.

Hilary brightened. "Yes!" she answered happily.

"Great attitude!" Dan beamed. "Now, *that's* what I like to hear. We can't let our Silver Blades skates get rusty!" He patted Hilary on the shoulder. "We've got auditions to ace! But before we get out there and give it our best, I'd like to lead you all in a little exercise."

"But Mr. Trapp—" Jill began.

"Dan," he corrected her. "You should all call me Dan. We're teammates, working together here."

Tori turned to Nikki. "He acts like we should be best friends with him, too!" she muttered, loud enough for everyone to hear.

Jill hesitated, waiting to see what Dan would say to Tori, but he just ignored her.

"Go on, Jill," he encouraged her. "What did you want to say?"

"Well, it's just that we all already have our own warm-up routines," she replied. "We've always done it like that."

"And you are still going to do that. Warm-ups are incredibly important to a good skating performance. Or for any sport, for that matter," he agreed. "But what I have in mind is something a little different."

Dan pulled his shoulders back and took a deep

breath. He rolled his neck and limbered his fingers, cracking his knuckles. Jill saw Tori wince at the sound.

"What I want to do is give you an exercise to help you work on your skating from the inside out," Dan continued. "You all know about the importance of mental attitude, right?"

"Sure," Haley responded, grinning from ear to ear.

"Good! Now, one of the ways that we can develop a winning mental attitude is with the support of our teammates," Dan said. "Especially now. Losing Mr. Weiler for a while is a big change. It's bound to be difficult for all of you. But together we can develop an edge to help us feel better. Even the best performers in the circus don't go out without a net! Why should you?"

He spread his hands comically as though he were trying to catch somebody falling from above him. A few kids began to giggle. Jill had to smile also. Dan definitely had a unique sense of humor.

"That's right," said Dan happily. "Loosen up! It feels good to laugh. Laughter is a good thing. It's a powerful healing agent. It chases away those distracting thoughts running around in your head. It sure is hard to skate well when you're worried about other things."

Dan paced back and forth in a circle.

"Believe me, I know how it is," he continued. "Distraction is your enemy. Think of it—you're just about to go for your big triple loop when out of the corner of your eye you see your friend Susie." Dan's voice shot up, high and whiny. "And you think, 'Why is Susie wearing that old thing again?' "

Everybody laughed.

"Or," he offered, speaking in a regular voice again, "it was a long day in school, and you just can't help thinking, 'I'm going to fail geometry if I didn't get that problem right on the exam.'"

There was a groan of recognition. Jill grinned at Patrick, and he looked back sympathetically. They both had a hard time with their math homework. Jill smiled at Dan. There *was* something likeable about him.

"We have to empty our minds of these thoughts. And we have to feel *good* on the ice," Dan told them. "We're here with our friends, we're having fun. Skating is *fun!*"

Dan paused and became more serious.

"When you're on the ice, you skate alone," he said gently. "Or, if you're a pairs skater, you skate with your partner. But it helps to know that when you're off the ice, you are not alone. We are a *team!*"

There were nods of agreement all around. Tori was still pouting stubbornly, but the other members of Silver Blades really seemed to have warmed up to Dan.

"So what I want now is for everybody to get in a big circle. Spread out," Dan instructed. "*Feel* the space. But don't get too far apart, because we're going to hold hands. I'm going to lead you in an exercise that will show you just what a team is about."

"I can't believe it." Tori tossed her head impatiently. "This is totally idiotic," she complained to Jill under her breath.

"It doesn't matter what you think now, it's how you're going to feel later," Dan assured Tori. He had obviously overheard her but he didn't seem mad. He motioned to Tori. "Why don't you come stand by me? What's your name?" he asked.

Tori raised her eyebrows haughtily. "Tori Carsen," she replied.

"You're one of my students. Great!" Dan said enthusiastically, smiling at Tori. "Come right over here. That's it."

Jill watched in amazement. Couldn't he tell that Tori was trying to be rude? she wondered.

Dan reached for Tori's hand as he continued explaining the exercise. "What we want to do next is take the hand of the persons to our left and right. Does everybody here have a left and a right hand?" he asked in mock seriousness.

The younger members of the club were getting a real case of the giggles. Dan reached for Hilary's hand on his other side.

"Be sure to hold on tight," Dan told them. "Close your eyes and take some deep breaths. On the fifth deep breath, I want you to lean way, way back. You're going to make a big arch. Try to reach your head to the floor behind you."

Everyone did as Dan instructed.

"And come back up," he said with an exaggerated groan.

As Jill returned to a standing position she felt a warm glow creep up her back and into her face.

"Now stretch at the waist as far to the right as you possibly can," Dan continued. "Feel your teammates' strength. Let them help pull you over there. Good. And now the same thing to the left. Reach—come on, go for it. Excellent!"

Jill was a little surprised at how much she liked the exercise. It was fun and it loosened her up, too.

"Okay, you can drop hands for a minute, but I want you to notice something," said Dan. "The teammates on either side of you kept you from falling backward during our big arch. And they brought you further in your side stretches than you would normally go on your own."

Tori coughed impatiently. Jill glanced her way and saw her give Dan a bored stare. I can't wait to see how he's going to coach her, Jill thought. She obviously can't stand him.

Jill glanced at Martina and Nikki, but their eyes were glued on Dan. They were both giving him their full attention, focused on every word he said. They were relaxed but concentrating. Nikki was smiling. They obviously are enjoying this, Jill remarked to herself. And I am, too. I guess Dan had a good idea, having us all warm up together like this.

"That's what a team does," Dan continued. "A team supports you and helps you reach for your best. As our final exercise, I want you to rejoin hands. Now look at every face in our circle. Memorize these faces. Close your eyes and see your team again. That's your backbone, your safety net, your strength. Use it!"

Tori let go of Dan's hand. Her face was set in a stubborn expression. "Having teammates is great," she said, "but let's get real. It's already Monday. We have less than two weeks to learn our *Nutcracker* routines. I mean, this is for a major audition! It's the worst possible time to lose our coach, even if it's only temporarily. How can teammates help with that?"

Dan studied Tori carefully. "You'd be surprised," he said simply. "But they can."

He clapped his hands energetically. "Tori is right about one thing, though—there's no time to lose!" Dan went on cheerfully, "So, let's go! Let's get ready for those auditions! Big lights! National TV! Your favorite stars—and Silver Blades! Get on that ice and skate!"

As everyone began to gather their things Dan pointed to Tori.

"Start your warm-up, Tori," he said. "I'll meet you in the center in one minute. We're going to be great together, you'll see." He winked.

Tori glared at him and stomped off. At least, as much as she could stomp in her skates, anyway, Jill thought with a little giggle.

Except for Tori, the Silver Blades teammates were a lot happier. They were certainly acting more bubbly than they had a few hours earlier, especially the younger skaters.

Jill glanced at Amber, who was heading out onto the ice to warm up.

This is no time to think about her, Jill told herself firmly. She made an effort to put the young skater out of her mind.

Like the coach said, Jill thought, it's time to skate!

10

It was Sunday morning. Jill had spent the past week skating hard, polishing her Clara routine—and worrying about Ryan. He used to call her every day. But she hadn't heard from him for a solid week. How could she *not* be worried?

Jill picked up the telephone and dialed Ryan's number. On the second ring she lost her nerve and slammed down the phone. Her heart was racing.

She needed to talk to somebody. Quickly she dialed Danielle's number. If anyone could help her, it was Dani.

"Jill!" Danielle sounded pleased to hear from her. "What's up?"

Jill sighed in relief. "Oh, Dani, I really need to talk to you! You have to help me."

"This is about Ryan, right?" Danielle laughed as Jill

gasped in surprise. "You have that worried-about-my-boyfriend wiggle in your voice."

Jill sank onto the kitchen chair. "You're right. I'm so upset. I haven't talked to him in a week. I just know he's mad at me about my skating!" She paused, taking a deep breath. "What if I had to choose between Ryan and a skating career? I mean, how did you do it? How did you decide to leave Silver Blades?"

There was a brief silence. "Jill, it was different for me," Danielle said carefully. "I just knew that writing was more important to me. But I can't believe you'd even dream of giving up skating!"

"I know," Jill wailed. "I *don't* want to! But I don't want to lose Ryan, either. What should I do? I'm putting in more practice time than ever. What if I never see him again?"

"Don't think that!" Danielle cried. "You're both really sensible. I'm sure you just need to talk this thing out. Until then, don't think the worst. You're probably wrong."

Jill chatted with Danielle a minute more, but she wasn't really listening. Danielle hadn't told her what she wanted to hear, and she was as worried as before. Sensible or not, she had no idea what to do about Ryan.

Jill grabbed her headphones off the kitchen counter and jammed them on, turning the music up loud. She didn't even want to think anymore. Suddenly she felt something grab her around the knees.

"Michael! Mark!" she shrieked. "When did you two sneak in?" She took off her headphones.

"We're going to go pick a Christmas tree! Right now!" Mark cried in excitement.

"Daddy said we could choose which one," Michael chimed in.

"Fantastic!" Jill said. It was just what she needed. She held out her hands to the twins, and they dragged her into the hall, nearly crashing into Kristi and Randi, who were jumping with their dolls off the stairs.

"You two know that you're not supposed to play on the stairs," Jill warned them gently. "You should take those toys to your room."

"But it's more fun here," Kristi objected. "See, we have a three-story house." She demonstrated the make-believe home.

"Nice," Jill agreed. "But right now it's cleanup time. And call Henry, too—we're going to get our Christmas tree."

"Hooray!" The girls scampered up the stairs to put away their toys.

The twins pulled Jill into the living room, where their father was trying to read the newspaper. Mark jumped on Mr. Wong's belly. Mr. Wong roared like a lion and started tickling both boys. Mrs. Wong came in carrying Laurie.

"Who's ready to go get our tree?" she asked.

"Tree time! Tree time!" the twins shouted together, jumping up and down.

Jill laughed. "I guess we all are," she said.

Mr. Wong put his newspaper aside with a chuckle. "Well, then, let's get this show on the road."

After everyone's coat, scarf, and mittens had been put on, the Wongs piled into their green minivan. Mr. Wong slipped behind the wheel and cleared his throat.

"Now, the tree farm we're going to belongs to one of my customers. We can choose any tree we like," he announced. "Mr. Chester was very kind to offer us a tree. The only catch is that we also have to chop it down ourselves."

"Does he have an axe for us to use?" Mrs. Wong asked.

"Yes, I believe he does," Mr. Wong replied with a twinkle. "It *is* a Christmas-tree farm, after all."

"I can't wait to see this," Henry joked.

"Boy, are you going to get a workout, Dad," Jill said.

Mr. Wong chuckled. "*You* may get the workout," he told Jill. "I always thought you and Henry would make great lumberjacks."

Everyone was excited and happy when they pulled up to Mr. Chester's tree farm. The snow on the ground made it look like something out of a fairy tale. The children's eyes opened wide.

"It looks magical here," Jill commented.

Jill helped her mother bundle Laurie in a blanket. Mr. Wong disappeared into a little shack off to one side of the entry gate. A few minutes later he was back, carrying a saw and an axe.

"Let's find that tree," he said.

Henry, Kristi, and Randi pelted each other with snowballs as the family searched through the snowy trees.

"That one's nice and bushy," Jill said, pointing at a short tree.

"No good," Mark cried. Michael nodded in agreement. "This one!" The twins both pointed at the same tree. It was not too tall and not too small, with a pretty, symmetrical shape. Mr. Wong beckoned Henry and Jill over. They began to saw and chop at the thick trunk. It was hard work. Finally the tree began to wobble.

"Timber!" Jill cried. The tree fell on its side with a soft whoosh.

The twins threw their arms around their father. Jill did the same, and so did Henry, Randi, and Kristi.

"It's a Wong Christmas sandwich," Mr. Wong said with a laugh.

Mrs. Wong's eyes grew misty with tears. "I look at this beautiful family and our beautiful tree and I know that no one could be happier than we are." She sighed loudly. "This is the best present anyone ever had."

Jill couldn't agree more.

"Now, who's dragging this tree back to the car?" Mr. Wong teased. "Are my lumberjacks ready?"

"Ready!" Jill and Henry exclaimed.

They got the tree back to the van. After a lot of huffing and puffing, Mr. Wong managed to tie it down to the roof. They returned the saw and the axe. Then the Wong family was on the road again.

Heading back home, Mr. Wong glanced at the dashboard. "We need some gas," he said.

They pulled into the next gas station. As Mr. Wong pumped gas Jill noticed a girl and a woman crossing the road. They looked very familiar. Jill cleared a spot on one of the fogged-up windows and squinted. Her mouth dropped open in surprise. It was Amber and her mother. And they were headed into the Seneca Hills Motel.

Could that be where Amber is staying? Jill wondered.

The cabins were all the same mousy brown, arranged in rows, one after the other. Jill doubted that many other kids were staying there.

"Hey, Mom," she said. "That place across the street. What's it like?"

"Oh, the motel?" Her mother peered out the window. "I've never been inside, but they say it's the best bargain in Seneca Hills."

"Bargain?" Jill repeated. "You mean it's cheap?"

"That's what I've heard," said Mrs. Wong. "It's perfectly clean and all that, but nothing fancy."

I wonder why Amber and her mother are staying *there*, Jill thought. She would have guessed that they were staying in a much nicer place, such as the Circle Tower Hotel.

"Why are you asking, sweetheart?" asked Mrs. Wong. She laughed. "You're not thinking of finding new accommodations, are you?"

"No, no," said Jill, laughing a little, too. "I was just curious, that's all."

As her father climbed back into the van, Jill gazed at the motel. It looked so lonely. What would it be like, staying in a motel with just your mom? Especially at

Christmas time. Jill couldn't imagine not being with her parents and brothers and sisters for the holiday.

A moment later Jill's father started the engine, and they took off. Jill put Amber out of her mind.

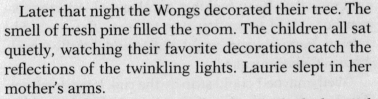

Later that night the Wongs decorated their tree. The smell of fresh pine filled the room. The children all sat quietly, watching their favorite decorations catch the reflections of the twinkling lights. Laurie slept in her mother's arms.

"We need more cookies," Jill announced. She hurried to the kitchen to refill a plate. As she entered the room the phone rang, and she went over to answer it.

"Hi, Jill," said the voice on the other end. "It's me, Ryan."

"Ryan!" Jill felt her heart speed up. "Um, how are you?"

"Okay, I guess," said Ryan. He paused. "Listen, I was thinking we should get together soon."

"Oh? I—I mean, sure, I guess so," Jill stammered.

"I know you're really busy with practice and stuff," Ryan said.

"Not so busy," Jill said quickly.

"But the auditions are coming up," Ryan said, sounding puzzled.

"They are," Jill agreed. "But I have *some* free time."

Ryan was quiet, and Jill hesitated.

"That was kind of funny," she finally said, "the way we bumped into each other at the mall." She tried to sound casual. "Did you get to do your errand, or whatever?"

"Um, yeah, I did," said Ryan. "That's one of the reasons I want to see you, Jill."

"Really?" Jill's throat tightened in panic. She was certain now that Ryan had met another girl. And the reason he wanted to see her was to break the news. She felt so nervous and upset she could hardly speak. "When?" she squeaked.

"Well, maybe I could stop by the rink later this week. Maybe you could take a few minutes off. We could go for another walk or something."

"Sure, okay." Later this week? Jill thought. It was a long time to wait. He must have bad news.

"How about Friday?" Ryan suggested.

Friday? Jill's stomach dropped. The day before the big auditions! It was a disaster.

"Uh, that's fine," said Jill, barely able to speak.

"Okay, then," said Ryan softly. "I'll tell you everything when I see you."

"All right." As Jill hung up the telephone a terrible feeling of despair welled up inside her.

She gazed through the door to the living room. Her family was gathered around the beautifully decorated tree. They all looked so happy.

Ryan can't break up with me now, she thought. How will I ever face Christmas?

The telephone rang again. Jill leaped at it.

"Hi, Jill," said the voice on the other end. "It's Tori!"

"Oh, Tori," Jill replied glumly. "How are you?"

"Okay, I guess," Tori answered. "What about you? You sound kind of down."

Jill thought a moment. She didn't really feel like telling Tori what had happened with Ryan. She decided to keep it to herself until she knew for sure. Besides, after what Tori had said at the mall, she would probably agree that Jill had something to worry about. The last thing Jill needed was to feel even worse.

"I'm okay," said Jill. "We went and chopped down a Christmas tree at a tree farm," she added, trying to sound enthusiastic.

"Chopped?" Tori repeated with amazement. "You mean with an *axe*?"

"Yeah. It was fun," Jill replied. "My dad has a customer who has a tree farm. He let us choose the tree we wanted. The house smells fantastic."

"Did you decorate it yet?" Tori asked.

"Yeah. It looks great! You have to come and see it," Jill said.

"I'd love to!"

"What about your tree?" Jill asked. "Have you gotten one yet?"

"We're supposed to go soon, maybe tomorrow," said Tori. "We always get ours at the Seneca Nursery. They trim it down so it's a perfect shape and deliver it and everything."

"Oh," said Jill. She couldn't imagine having a tree that had been trimmed to a perfect shape. "What's up?" she asked, changing the subject.

"It's that awful Dan Trapp!" Tori complained. "I can't stand working with him."

Jill wasn't surprised. "I could tell you weren't exactly impressed," she said.

"And I'm not the only one," Tori said. "My mother is so annoyed, you wouldn't believe it."

Oh, yes I would, Jill said to herself. "What did she say?" she asked Tori.

"She thinks it's absolutely ridiculous to spend so much practice time talking instead of skating. And I agree with her completely. All that positive-thinking stuff," Tori huffed. "We all know that working on the Clara program is *the* most important thing. The scouts will be here at the end of the week!"

"I know," said Jill. "But a lot of people liked what Dan had to say."

"Oh, *really*." Tori sighed. "You and I are practically the best skaters in the club. We didn't get to be so good by spending all our time working on the skater from the inside out, like Dan is always saying."

"You might have a point," Jill admitted. She was flattered by Tori's compliment, but she also wasn't sure that Dan's ideas were completely wrong.

"Of *course* I'm right," Tori snapped. "I think we should get rid of him. I want Mr. Weiler back. He's a much better coach than Dan Trapp will ever be."

"But Mr. Weiler's still very sick," Jill pointed out. "It

doesn't sound like he'll be back anytime soon. Silver Blades needs a substitute coach. I mean, Kathy can't coach everybody."

"Well, I don't care. There are other coaches in the world. And I have a great idea," Tori announced.

"What's that?" Jill asked.

"I'm starting a petition to get rid of Dan. I'm going to get everybody to sign it. Then they'll *have* to find someone else. Maybe they'll even let Blake be a coach. Will you sign?" Tori asked eagerly.

Jill hesitated. "I'll have to think about it."

"What's there to think about?" Tori argued. "If it was a petition to get rid of Amber, I bet you'd sign in a second."

"Tori!" Jill laughed in surprise. "Amber drives me crazy, but I wouldn't go *that* far."

"Well, I would," Tori declared. "If someone followed me around everywhere, asking a million nosy questions, I'd get rid of them for sure." Tori paused. "By the way, is she still asking you a million questions?"

"Yeah, sometimes," Jill admitted.

"What? When?" Tori pressed.

"Well, like the other day, just before the call about Mr. Weiler," Jill said. "Kathy was helping me with my layback. The minute Kathy left, Amber asked me to tell her everything that Kathy said." Jill felt a flicker of annoyance, remembering the incident. "She had a lot of nerve. It was my practice time, not show and tell," she added.

"Wow. That's not very professional," Tori said. "And

you know, I heard her grilling Blake about the Clara routine. She practically made him teach her the whole thing. I can't stand it! She's always pushing her way into everything. Why doesn't she just go away and leave us all alone?"

"I know," Jill agreed. "Amber could just ask Kathy for help with her layback. After all, she has Kathy's last time slot."

Tori gasped. "Oh, so *that's* why Kathy can't coach me!" she snapped angrily. "Because she's taken on Amber!"

Jill drew in a deep breath. She hadn't meant to let that slip. Suddenly Jill felt guilty about gossiping. "Well, it was Kathy's decision," she said.

"Maybe. But it doesn't mean my mother and I can't make Kathy change her mind," Tori said with determination. "It's not fair. Amber's not even in Silver Blades! I can't believe the way she's taking over!"

And I can't believe I opened my big mouth, Jill thought with a pang. Now Tori's going to get even more upset about the whole thing. And Mrs. Carsen, too.

For some reason Jill suddenly remembered the sad image of Amber going home to the Seneca Hills Motel. Jill was surprised, but she felt sorry for Amber.

"Well, remember," Jill added quickly, "Amber has a lot of potential. That's why Kathy wants to work with her."

"*I'm* a good skater, too," Tori said, sounding very annoyed. "I have lots of talent. And *I'm* a member of Silver Blades. That ought to count for *something*!"

"Of course it does," Jill assured her. "Anyway, try not to think about it. Not this week. Just focus on the auditions. That's the most important thing."

"Now you sound like Dan!" Tori groaned. "He's always saying things like that. 'It's the skating that counts,'" she said, imitating the coach.

"But he's right about that," Jill said thoughtfully. "Listen, Tori, I have to hang up. I still have homework before I go to bed. And you know how much I hate homework." Jill sighed. "I'll see you at the rink tomorrow, okay?"

"Okay, Jill," Tori answered. "Good night. See you tomorrow."

"Good night, Tori." Jill hung up.

I wish I hadn't talked so much, Jill thought. I mean, sure, I don't like Amber, either. But I should have remembered that anything I tell Tori will be all over the rink tomorrow—if not all over Seneca Hills!

11

Friday morning Jill crowded into the locker room with everyone else. It felt as though every single member of Silver Blades was rushing to get dressed at once. All anyone could talk about was *Nutcracker on Ice*. The scouts were due the next day! Silver Blades was the last club the scouts needed to see. When their auditions were over, the scouts would decide who had a part in the ice show and who didn't. Knowing that they would find out the results of their auditions right away added to the pressure. Tension and excitement filled the air like electricity.

Haley slid over to make room for Jill on the locker room bench. "I am so nervous!" Haley exclaimed. "I can't believe we have only two practices before the auditions. All I could think about all week was nutcrackers and mice!"

Jill knew what Haley meant. She had eaten, slept, and skated Clara for the last week. Her mind was focused on the auditions. She hadn't let herself think about anything else—because when she did, worries about Ryan crowded her mind.

She was going to see him that afternoon. She was so nervous about it that she wished Dan would do some of his positive-thinking exercises with her right then and there. "Ryan won't break up with you," Dan would say. "And you will win the role of Clara." Instead Jill took several deep breaths to calm down. She had to get ready for practice.

She had just finished braiding her hair when Danielle entered the locker room.

"Dani," Jill said in surprise. "What are you doing here? The auditions are tomorrow morning!"

"I know," Danielle answered. "But I need background on what happens *before* the scouts come."

Jill grabbed Danielle's arm and leaned close so no one would hear. "Dani, Ryan's coming to talk to me this afternoon," she whispered. "I'm so nervous! And I can't be nervous. I need to skate my best today, not my worst!"

Danielle patted Jill's arm. "Relax. Everything will work out. I know it will."

Before Jill could say anything more, Tori rushed up to Danielle. "I'm so excited about your article," Tori exclaimed. "Do you want to interview me?"

"Later, Tori," Danielle said. "Right now I just need background notes." Danielle sighed happily. "This will be my second cover story, you know. Another article that'll say 'by Danielle Panati.' And right on the front page!" Her eyes sparkled.

"Good for you," Haley called as she pulled on black leggings. She knotted a huge pink T-shirt at her waist and scrunched up a pair of hot-pink socks. "But what made them decide to let you do the story, Dani?"

"You mean besides the fact that I am *the* perfect writer for it?" Danielle joked. "To tell you the truth, I think it was two things. First Mr. Weiler had his heart attack. And then Dan Trapp came to be his replacement. That made it front-page news."

Jill was astonished. "Wasn't it enough that we might be on national television with Trisha McCoy and Christopher Kane?" she asked.

Danielle grinned. "As much as I love you guys, the paper hardly ever runs a sports story on the cover."

"I'm glad it's a break for you," Nikki told her.

Danielle blushed slightly. "Thanks," she said. "But enough about me. You guys are the stars. And I'll keep my fingers crossed for all of you." She pulled a notebook out of the back pocket of her faded jeans, flipped it open, and scribbled something.

Tori sauntered casually over to Danielle and tried to read her notes over her shoulder. Danielle turned.

"Tori, I don't think you'll find this too interesting," she said. "I just wrote down the date." She grinned. "I won't leave you out, I promise."

"Say, I have an idea, Dani," Haley said. "You could write about how much Tori likes her new coach, Dan Trapp."

Jill covered her mouth with her hand to stifle a laugh.

"Please!" Tori exclaimed, rolling her eyes. "I don't want to talk about Dan Trapp. When my mom shows up, we're going to go see Kathy about him. But I'd better go. I can't be late. The last thing I need is one of Dan's lectures about how I should be more *enthusiastic*." She sailed out of the locker room.

"What's that all about?" Danielle asked, puzzled.

"Tori can't stand working with Dan," Jill answered. "She hates all his positive thinking and his idea about working on a skater from the inside out. He's way different from Mr. Weiler. It's hard for Tori to get used to him. But I think he's pretty good."

"He's been really helpful to me and Patrick," Haley agreed. "He used to skate pairs himself, you know. I like him almost as much as Mr. Weiler."

"Speaking of being late," Jill said, "I've got to go, too. See you all later!"

"Oh, Jill, wait!" Nikki called. "I'm running to the mall after practice later. Do you still want that red headband for the auditions tomorrow? Last chance!"

Jill frowned. She had wanted the headband. She'd loved it the minute she tried it on. But once Amber had put it on her own head, Jill didn't want to have anything more to do with it. She *hated* that headband now.

"No, thanks, Nikki. I changed my mind. I'd rather not spend the money. See you on the ice!"

Jill glided over to her practice area. The first thing she noticed was Kathy coaching Amber on her layback. Jill tried to push Amber out of her mind. She had to focus on her warm-ups.

As she stretched her hamstrings she heard Tori speaking angrily to Dan. Jill strained to hear what Tori was saying. It was clear that Tori was complaining.

Jill ran through each portion of the Clara program. It went well, but she wasn't having fun. She felt irritated each time she glanced at Kathy and Amber. It seemed that Kathy heaped attention on the younger skater. She doesn't compliment *me* like that, Jill thought, watching as Kathy nodded and smiled at Amber. Jill turned away and worked on her double axel.

After some more practice on the jump, Jill decided it was time to work on improving *her* layback, too. Across the rink, Kathy had her hand in the small of Amber's back. She was busy explaining where her arch should be located.

Amber nodded and tried the move again. Jill couldn't help noticing that Amber did the spin better and better each time. Better than Jill herself, even. I can't stand this, Jill thought. The scouts are coming tomorrow. Why is Kathy coaching Amber? She should be working with *me*!

As Jill worked on her layback again she heard Tori arguing with Dan. Tori sounded really upset, but Dan was talking to her patiently.

Tori's voice rose. Jill could hear every word.

"Dan, if you tell me to work on my skating from the inside out one more time, I'm going to scream!" Tori yelled.

"Tori, being angry with me is only getting in your

way," Dan responded. "You're a terrific skater, but we're making you even better."

"What's going to make me better is going over my jumps again," Tori wailed. "I'm still not landing the triple toe loop every time. What if I blow it for the scouts? I'll never get a part!"

"Try not to think about the scouts. If you focus on them, you won't be able to skate as well. On the other hand," Dan went on, "if you feel relaxed and have a good time, the skating will flow out of you naturally, and you'll look like a million bucks for the scouts. Trust me. I know what I'm talking about."

"I don't think you *do* know what you're talking about," Tori said rudely. "Mr. Weiler would be helping me land the triple toe loop. You just want to *talk*. It's ridiculous!"

"Tori, we've done a lot of work on the triple, and you know it," Dan said without a trace of anger in his voice. "You've improved quite a bit."

"But not enough!" Tori retorted.

"I agree. That's what we're working on," Dan replied. "Now, just take a deep breath. Picture yourself landing a perfect triple toe loop. You can do it, I know you can."

Tori heaved a big sigh, but she took her starting position. She powered around the rink, then lifted her body into the jump. After two revolutions, she fell with a thud. She glared at Dan as she brushed ice from her cream-colored tights.

"You weren't very focused on the jump," Dan corrected her. "Try it again, and try to imagine that you can do the jump with ease. Use your strength. Be positive!"

"There's only one thing I'm positive about!" Tori exploded. "You're not my coach anymore! I'm not taking any more of this! And that's final!"

Tori sped away from Dan. She skated up to Kathy.

"Kathy, this is *really* important," Tori declared. "You have to coach me. I can't work with Dan anymore!"

"Tori," Kathy objected, "you know that I'm booked solid. I can't coach you. You have to learn to work with Dan. He's an excellent coach. Just give him a chance."

"I tried," Tori insisted. "It's impossible."

"Tori, please. I expect you to make some adjustments while Mr. Weiler is out, just like I expect the rest of the club to do," Kathy said. "Do your best."

"You could have time for me if you wanted to," Tori said angrily. "But you want to work with *her*." Tori pointed at Amber.

Jill saw Amber turn pale. The young skater stared down at the ice, her shoulders hunched.

"*We're* the ones who have the audition tomorrow. You should be working with *us*!" Tori insisted.

Tori has a point, Jill agreed silently. Kathy *should* be working with us, not Amber. She just wished Tori wouldn't be so pushy and rude about it. She knew Kathy wouldn't let her get away with that.

"Tori," Kathy said sharply, "I am the coach. I decide how to use my coaching time. You need to listen to Dan, not disrupt an important practice session. You know better than that. Now go back and work on your program."

Jill could see that Kathy was trying to hold back her temper. But Tori couldn't seem to stop herself.

"I am not going to work with Dan!" Tori said in a fury.

"Tori, your behavior is unacceptable," Kathy said quietly. "Take a break and think this over calmly."

"I don't need to think anything over!" Tori yelled. "I already know what to do. I won't work with Dan. And since you won't coach me, there's only one thing I *can* do." Tori paused to take a deep breath. "I'm leaving!" she announced. "I quit!"

Tori skated off the ice, slamming into the boards on her way out. Without a backward glance, she stomped into the locker room.

Jill couldn't believe it. As she stared after Tori a stunned silence settled over the ice. Tori *has* to come back, Jill thought.

Minutes went by, and Tori didn't reappear. Jill began to worry that Tori really meant it. She could be awfully stubborn.

"All right, everybody, back to work," Kathy said sternly.

Reluctantly Jill started her practice again. She tried to improve her layback. But she couldn't stop thinking about Tori. I can't believe she did that, Jill thought, biting her lip. After all the hard work we've done together and everything, Tori can't quit now . . . can she?

～ ～

Jill had just finished running through the Clara routine when Ryan entered the rink. Quietly he found a seat in the stands. Jill gasped in surprise. He was supposed to meet her at afternoon practice! Her heart began to beat faster. Was he so anxious to break up with her that he couldn't wait?

Somehow Jill forced herself to complete her double Lutz–double loop jump combination. She wobbled uneasily into the layback to finish.

She glanced over at Kathy, who was coaching Amber on the other side of the ice. For once she was relieved that Kathy was paying attention to Amber instead of her. If Kathy had seen that finish, she definitely would have made Jill try it again. And the way Jill was feeling, she doubted she'd be able to do much better. With Ryan sitting only a few yards away, Clara's jumps for joy seemed impossible.

Ryan gave Jill a little wave. Jill felt sick to her stomach. Well, I have to get it over with sooner or later, she decided.

Taking a deep breath to calm her nerves, she skated over to the stands.

"Hi," said Ryan as Jill stepped off the ice.

"Hi." Jill could barely get the word out.

"I know our date was for later, but I couldn't wait," Ryan burst out. "Is now an okay time for us to take that walk?"

"Sure," said Jill. "Let me put on my shoes."

She hurried into the locker room. A few moments later she was back, wearing her sneakers and parka. As they walked silently out the door of the arena, Jill thought how she would feel once things with Ryan were really over. Tears welled up in her eyes, and she had to bite her lip to hold them back.

They wandered down the path in silence. Finally Ryan stopped and turned to her.

"Jill," he said, looking at her with concern, "I'm really worried. Is everything okay with you?"

"With *me*?" Jill repeated in surprise.

"Well, sure," said Ryan. "I mean, you've been acting kind of funny lately."

"*I've* been acting funny?" Jill said in bewilderment. "What are you talking about?"

"Well, for a while now you've seemed kind of . . . I don't know, just not as friendly as you usually are," Ryan explained. "Even today. Ever since I got here I've had this feeling that you're not happy to see me."

"I've just been afraid that *you're* not happy to see *me*!" Jill burst out.

"What do you mean?" asked Ryan, looking confused.

"Well, everything," Jill cried. "You've been acting strange for the past two weeks. Like that day I ran into you in the mall," she began. "You were so weird with me. And then you didn't call me all week, and . . ." Her voice trailed off.

"I'm sorry," said Ryan. "But I thought you were busy practicing. And it's just that—"

"I know you're upset about my skating," Jill interrupted. Now that she had started talking, she couldn't stop. "I know I spend a lot of time at practice. I know I don't have as much time for you as another girl might, and . . . and I'm sorry, too . . . and—" Jill burst into tears.

"Jill!" Ryan put an arm around her shoulders.

"I didn't know what to do!" Jill cried. "I just couldn't choose between you and skating, but—"

"Hold on," Ryan said. "Choose between what? I don't want you to give up skating."

Jill wiped her eyes. "You don't?"

"No," Ryan said. "I'm proud of your skating." He grinned suddenly. "Wow—you really thought about giving up skating for *me*?"

"Well, yeah. But I don't understand." Jill drew in a deep breath. "Don't you want me to choose? You seemed so upset when I couldn't see you that Sunday. And I know you were unhappy about the whole *Nutcracker* audition thing."

Ryan glanced down at his feet. "Well," he said slowly, "you're right about one thing. I *was* kind of upset about the auditions. But not because you were skating too much." Ryan looked directly into Jill's eyes.

"I had all these ideas about spending Christmas with you," he went on. "And you were excited about being *gone*. You see, I had just made special plans for us."

"Special plans?" Jill repeated.

Ryan nodded. "I had it all figured out. We were going to take a moonlight sleigh ride the night before Christmas Eve."

"A moonlight sleigh ride?" said Jill excitedly.

"Yeah, with horses and jingle bells and everything," Ryan told her with a bashful smile.

"That sounds wonderful!"

"I wanted to surprise you," he explained. "But the guy who has the sleigh said that the rides get booked up really fast around Christmas, so I had to make reservations early. Then you said you might be away that day. I was really disappointed. It was as if you'd forgotten me completely."

"Oh, Ryan," Jill said in a choked voice. "I feel terrible."

She *had* been excited about the possibility of going to Boston to tape the *Nutcracker* ice show. She hadn't stopped to worry about being away from Ryan right before Christmas.

"I mean," Ryan continued, "of course I was happy for you. This could be a great opportunity. But I knew I could never come up with another Christmas surprise as good as that."

"It was a great idea," said Jill, her heart melting.

"So that's what I was doing at the mall that day," Ryan went on. "Looking for a different present for you. I wanted to find something else really special. I know I acted strange when you and your friends saw me coming out of Canady's. I was afraid you'd guess that I was shopping for you."

"That's all it was?" Jill shook her head in amazement. "You don't want another girlfriend? You don't want to break up with me?"

Ryan looked shocked. "Of course not!"

Jill smiled at him warmly. "Oh, Ryan, I'm so happy! I can't believe you were shopping for my present!"

"Yeah, well, unfortunately I couldn't find anything that seemed right," said Ryan. "I had every salesperson in the place helping me out, but nothing seemed special enough."

"That's okay," said Jill. Sure, she thought, a present from Ryan would be great, but the most important thing was that she had *him*.

Ryan smiled. He reached out and gently brushed Jill's bangs off her face. "I never want to break up with you," he whispered. "Listen, Jill, I can't wait. Do you mind if I give you your present right now?"

"My present? Mind? N-No," Jill stammered. She was just so relieved that Ryan still liked her—how could she mind *anything*? "But you just said that you couldn't find me a present."

Ryan dug into his coat pocket. "Luckily I did find something special somewhere else," he said. He pulled out a small red box tied with a white ribbon. "I hope you like it." He handed the box to Jill.

Jill untied the ribbon carefully and opened the box. Inside was a bracelet made of delicate gold hearts linked together to form a chain.

"Oh, wow," Jill gasped. "I can't believe it. Thank you, Ryan." She raised her eyes to his. "It's beautiful."

Ryan gazed back at her.

"So are you," he said softly. Then he bent down to give her a gentle kiss.

12

It was Saturday. Finally the day of the big auditions had arrived. Jill gazed happily around the Seneca Hills Ice Arena. The snowy expanse of ice gleamed under the bright lights. She could hardly wait for the scouts to arrive. Now that everything was settled with Ryan, her mind was free from worry. She was really looking forward to skating the Clara program.

Haley arrived and linked her arm through Jill's. "This is it," Haley said, her eyes twinkling with excitement. "I guess everyone else is in the locker room, huh?"

Jill nodded. "I just wanted to stay out here a minute."

"Not to watch Amber," Haley teased.

The ice was empty except for Amber. Since she was the only one not auditioning, she was using the time to work out. With the ice all to herself, she was really flying around.

"No," Jill admitted, laughing. "I wanted to be here in case the scouts showed up."

"Me too," Haley said. "It helps to know who you're skating for."

Just then the four scouts arrived. Haley and Jill only glimpsed the two men and two women as they headed into the office with Kathy and Dan. One man was short and balding. He looked very stern. The other man was tall with gray hair. He wore a shirt and a tie under his navy blue blazer. One woman was slim and tall, with dark hair cut short. The other woman wore her dark blond hair pulled back in a ponytail.

Jill and Haley dashed back into the locker room to give a report.

"Well?" Martina asked. "Did you see them?"

"We sure did," Jill answered.

"Of course," Haley retorted. "When we go out on a mission, we get the job done!"

"So?" Nikki urged. "Who are they?"

"There's two women and two men," Jill said. "It was hard to tell much about them from so far away. They're in the office with Kathy and Dan."

"I still can't believe that Tori isn't here," Haley said sadly. "I talked to her all last night, trying to get her to change her mind. But she said she definitely won't come back."

"I can't imagine the club without her." Jill sighed. "How could her mother let her quit?"

"It's pretty strange, considering Mrs. Carsen's such a skating mom and all," Haley agreed. "I don't know what to think about it." She shook her head. "Anyway, good luck to you, Jill."

Jill met Haley's eyes. She flushed. Jill knew what Haley was thinking. Jill and Tori were the best singles skaters in Silver Blades. With Tori gone, Jill had no real competition for the role of Clara. Of course, the scouts had seen other skaters at other clubs. One of them might have already impressed them. Even so, one less skater as competition made Jill's chances even stronger.

Okay, Jill told herself, forget about Tori. Forget about the other skaters. Just get out there and skate your best.

She zipped up her best red and black velvet skating dress. It flared beautifully over her hips. She tugged it down and pulled on cream-colored wool tights. Her hair was twisted in a special French braid.

Danielle stuck her head into the locker room. "Mind if I come in?" she asked.

"No, Dani, come on," Jill answered.

"I might just know a thing or two that would interest you," Danielle teased. She turned to the mirror and straightened the collar of her pink blouse. She caught Jill's eyes on her and smiled.

"Okay, Dani," Jill said. "Come on, tell us. What did you find out?"

"Just who some of those scouts are," Danielle said.

"Really?" Nikki whirled around. "Tell us! Who are they?"

"How did you find out?" asked Martina.

"Oh, we reporters have our sources," Danielle said mysteriously.

"You know how nervous we are, and you're teasing us!" Jill said with a laugh.

"No, really," Danielle said sincerely. "I grabbed Dan when he stepped out of the office to get coffee from the snack bar. The blond woman is Kirsti Johansson."

"Isn't she a Swedish singles skater?" Haley asked.

"Yes, I think so," Danielle answered. She looked at her notes. "And one of the men is Tom Wright, a former competition judge. The other man is Fred Tannenbaum. He's the producer of the entire ice show." She looked up, pleased with herself. "Being a reporter has its advantages!"

"Thanks for telling us, Dani," Jill said. "But I'm still totally nervous."

"We all are," Nikki agreed. "I have butterflies in my stomach that just won't quit."

"Speaking of quitting," Danielle asked quietly, "has Tori shown up yet?"

"No. And we don't expect her to," Haley reported. "She told me last night that she's definitely not coming to the auditions."

"Wow. It's hard to believe," Danielle replied. Then she brightened, throwing an arm around Haley's shoulder. "But you look great! Is that a new outfit?"

"Yes. It's no big deal, but I needed something." She gestured to her short navy blue jacket with gold buttons and a skirt to match. "Patrick and I thought we'd wear matching uniforms." Haley gave a salute, and everyone laughed.

Nikki smoothed her white chiffon skating dress. She took a final look in the mirror and announced, "I guess I'm ready. What do you think?"

Jill nodded approvingly. "You look fantastic, Nikki. Very elegant."

"The scouts will be impressed with all of you," Danielle added.

"I hope you're right," Jill said. "*All* of us look pretty great, if I do say so myself. Or at least I will when I fix this hair." Jill tucked up a loose end of her French braid. The delicate gold chain on Jill's wrist caught the light.

"Oh, Jill, I just love the bracelet that Ryan gave you," Danielle told her.

Jill had shown the bracelet to everyone the day before. By now they all knew about the mix-up between her and Ryan.

"Thanks," said Jill, blushing a little.

Nikki's eyes sparkled. "It's so romantic, the way things ended up okay for you guys."

"I'm really happy for you two," Danielle added.

Jill smiled. "Ryan's so great! The only trouble is, now I'll *really* miss him—if I get to go to Boston, that is."

Martina sighed. "I wish someone would give *me* a sleigh ride. Especially if I end up staying here instead of going to Boston." She glanced down at her pastel pink dress with its line of pearl buttons down the front to the waist. "I thought this looked like something

Clara would wear," she said a little shyly. "But I know I probably won't be chosen for the part. My triple toe loop is hopeless. But if I'm lucky, I could still be a mouse or something."

"Keep a positive attitude, Martina," Haley said, sounding just like Dan. "I'm sure you'll do fine."

"Thanks, Haley," Martina said appreciatively. "It is pretty exciting even getting to audition. I love being in Silver Blades. I guess that's why I don't understand Tori. She really loves this club."

"Maybe something will happen," Haley said, but she sounded doubtful.

Jill finished off her braid with new red velvet ribbons. Okay, she thought, looking at herself in the mirror. Now if I can only do well with my program . . .

She closed her eyes and ran the series of jumps and spins through her mind. It seemed like the millionth time she'd rehearsed this way.

You can do this, Jill told herself. Remember—enjoy yourself.

She thought back to the first day of working on the role of Clara. She remembered how much she'd felt as though she actually *were* Clara.

Jill held that image in her mind and fingered her bracelet for good luck. I'm ready, she thought.

As the girls left the locker room and approached the rink, Jill gave a gasp of surprise. Amber was still on the ice.

Not only that, but she was running flawlessly through the Clara program! She wasn't even supposed to know the program, but there she was, skating it in front of the scouts!

And the scouts were watching her!

Jill couldn't believe it. On top of everything, Amber was dressed from head to toe in *red*.

Jill stared at Amber, horrified.

How could she do this to me? Jill thought as angry tears stung her eyelids. Not only is she trying to take my part away, but she's actually imitating me! Everyone knows that red is my color.

Haley bumped into Jill from behind. "Am I seeing what I think I'm seeing?" she said. "She's doing the Clara part!"

Danielle crowded next to them. "Wow. She's amazing," Danielle said. "I've never seen her skate before."

Jill frowned. "But it's not right, Dani. She's performing the Clara program for the scouts and she's not even a member of Silver Blades."

Danielle was quick to agree. "I'm surprised Kathy let her do it." She paused. "And how could she wear your color?"

"It's obvious," Jill said sharply. "First she follows me around. Then she asks a million questions and copies my moves in practice. And now this! I'm surprised she isn't wearing the headband I tried on at the mall!"

"That velvet one?" Nikki asked. "Why do you say that?"

"It's not important. It's just that when we passed the store again, Amber was trying it on," Jill answered.

The longer Jill watched Amber skate, the angrier she

became. She stared at Amber's red outfit. It didn't even match well. It was actually a bunch of different red things thrown together.

Jill glanced at the scouts. Kirsti Johansson didn't take her eyes off Amber for a second. Jill wasn't sure which man was the former judge and which one was the producer, but they were both smiling approvingly and making quiet comments to each other.

Finally Amber prepared for the final jump, the double Lutz–double loop. She performed it perfectly. She even *acted* the part of Clara, smiling as though she was jumping for joy. Amber ended the routine with a perfect layback—the move that Kathy had been coaching her on.

As soon as the young girl finished Kathy stepped forward. She faced the waiting group of Silver Blades skaters.

"I'd like to make a brief announcement before we begin the auditions," she said. "Amber Armstrong is joining Silver Blades. I know you'll all welcome her to the club. She's a great addition to our team."

Amber? A member of Silver Blades?

Jill was stunned. It was the worst news she could imagine!

13

Amber skated off the ice. When she got to the boards she turned around and looked straight at Jill. She gave a little wave and a smile.

Jill stared back at her. Amber was in Silver Blades. Amber could audition for the role of Clara. It was no accident that she had skated the part in front of the scouts. She wasn't practicing—she was auditioning.

Jill felt sick to her stomach. Had Kathy known all along? Had she planned to let Amber audition that way? It seemed so sneaky. Yet Amber was good, Jill realized. And since she was a Silver Blades skater now, why wouldn't Kathy want her to be up for the part?

Jill gritted her teeth. Only one skater could be Clara, and Jill was determined to be the one.

This part means too much to me, Jill told herself. The

Clara role is my ticket back to the Academy! No one is going to take that chance away from me.

"All right, everybody," Kathy announced, "it's time for warm-ups. Then we'll go straight into the auditions. Let's get on the ice!"

Jill noticed that Kathy and Dan seemed happy and excited about the auditions. That made her feel better. The two coaches appeared to have a lot of confidence in *all* the skaters.

Jill focused on her warm-up. She made herself feel each muscle and tendon loosen up. She forced herself to clear her mind of any thoughts that might distract her.

Don't think about anything except how great it feels to skate Clara, she told herself firmly.

Before she knew it, warm-ups were over. It was time for the auditions to begin. Jill felt confident and relaxed as she waited for her turn.

The scouts had decided to review the pairs skaters first. Dan talked quietly to each pair before they went out on the ice. Jill had to smile at the way he encouraged his skaters. He really does care about us, Jill thought appreciatively.

Haley and Patrick were first. The music began. There was a gentle murmur of violins. Then a flute joined in. Last, there was the chiming of bells. Haley and Patrick waltzed onto the ice together. The gold buttons on Haley and Patrick's matching jackets flashed against the navy blue background. With their red hair, they made a striking picture.

From the waltz step they moved smoothly into side-by-side flying camels. Haley and Patrick smiled widely at each other. They really seemed to enjoy skating the program together.

The music became more driving, with the violins setting the pace. They did a pair sit spin. Then they powered around the rink with backward crossovers. They floated through a matched set of flying splits. They performed side-by-side double salchows and an axel. Then Patrick danced around Haley while she did a perfect layback spin.

The closing included a line of intricate footwork leading into a graceful death spiral. Jill knew that Haley and Patrick had worked long and hard on the spin. They performed it perfectly and came to a beautiful finish.

Jill could tell that the scouts were pleased with the performance. They took a lot of notes after Patrick and Haley left the ice. Jill crossed her fingers for her friends.

Nikki and Alex went next. Everything went smoothly, except that Jill could see how hard they were both concentrating. Their skating was fine, but it seemed to Jill that they were trying very hard not to make any mistakes. It made their skating look stiff and tense, especially compared to Patrick and Haley, who had made the routine look fun.

The next pair to come out was Josh Buskirk skating with Christine Rosenblum. Jill was curious to watch them. She knew that they hadn't been skating together for very long, so the program was going to be hard for them.

Seeing Josh skate reminded Jill of Tori. She remembered how well Josh and Tori had skated in the Silver Blades Ice Spectacular the year before. It made Jill sadder than ever that Tori hadn't shown up for the auditions.

And Jill had to admit that Christine was no match for Tori. Josh and Christine's program was not the best. Josh almost dropped Christine in the star lift, and they left out the death spiral altogether.

Not a good sign, Jill noted to herself. Skaters often left out the more challenging parts of a program if they were unsure of themselves, even though doing something like substituting a double jump for a triple counted against them. Still, it was better than falling on the ice or dropping someone. At least singles skaters didn't have to worry about harming their partner.

Jill glanced at her watch. When would it be time for her to skate Clara? She was starting to feel more nervous.

Kathy had told Jill that she would be the last singles skater to audition. Jill was used to coming at the end. Having a family name that began with *W* meant that she went last a lot.

Jill glanced at Danielle. She was busy taking notes for her article. Danielle saw Jill watching and gave her a thumbs-up sign for good luck.

Finally the auditions for the singles skaters began. Jill focused her attention on her friends' performances.

She watched for any difficulties the others had so that she could avoid making similar mistakes.

It was Martina's turn to perform. She looked very nervous as she stepped out onto the ice. Jill held her breath as Martina moved into the opening triple toe loop. Martina always had so much trouble with the jump!

Her preparation looked solid, and Jill thought she was off to a good start. But suddenly Martina tensed. Halfway through her last rotation it was clear she didn't have the height she needed to move into a smooth landing, and she thudded to the ice. Jill winced. She could imagine how awful Martina felt.

But Martina jumped up quickly. She brushed the snow off her tights and continued skating. She managed to complete her audition calmly. Still, as she glided off the ice Jill saw tears in her eyes.

Martina was not nearly as strong a skater as Jill. She had never been real competition for the role of Clara. But Jill understood how Martina was feeling right now, and her heart ached for her friend. There was no time to think about that now, though. Suddenly it was Jill's turn!

When Jill heard her name called she made an effort to clear her mind. She went over her opening moves one last time. Then she glided to the center of the rink. When she was ready she raised her arms to the start position. Breathe, she reminded herself. Focus, and breathe.

The music started. Jill felt a smile spread across her

face. She loved *The Nutcracker*! As she began her opening move, she found herself forgetting all about the audition and the scouts. She felt as though she were Clara
again, leaping with joy as she received the nutcracker
and showed it to all the Christmas guests.

Jill seemed to float into the triple toe loop. Her body
lifted effortlessly, and she completed the rotations eas-
ily, landing smoothly. Without any effort, she lightly
bounced into a series of delicate waltz jumps.

Then she powered once around the rink, moving eas-
ily to the music. She really felt Clara's happiness as she
leaped into the double axel. She landed with precision
and grace and immediately launched into the flying
camel.

Centering her spin, Jill kept the rotation in exactly
the same place on the ice. She held her arms out perfectly straight from her body, with her chin lifted. She
felt great. A dazzling smile spread across her face.

At the close of the program she flew over the ice in
a series of crossovers before landing the double Lutz–
double loop combination. When she spun into her final
layback, Jill felt exactly as Clara was supposed to feel
in the scene. It was truly a moment of quiet happiness
and satisfaction.

Jill couldn't have been more pleased with her performance. As she skated off the ice Kathy and Dan
beamed at her. Kathy even reached over and gave her
a quick hug. Jill was thrilled that she had skated so
well.

She glanced over at the scouts. They were huddled

together in a conference. Then they all glanced at Jill. The tall man gave her a smile while the other scouts wrote some notes. Jill hoped they were impressed.

Meanwhile, Danielle, Nikki, and Haley skated up to her. Danielle gave her an especially big hug.

"You were fantastic," Danielle cried. "That's the best I've seen you skate since you broke your foot."

"I thought so, too," Haley added.

"Thanks, guys," Jill said, blushing a little bit. "I hope the scouts agree with you." She had her fingers crossed for luck. I really, really, want this, she chanted silently. This proves that I'm ready to go back to the Academy, Jill thought. I'm as good—no, I'm better than I was before!

She glanced at her friends' faces. Their praise meant a lot. Jill blushed again, remembering how badly she'd treated them before. When she came home for vacation from the Academy, she had acted like a big hotshot. Her friends forgave her. Then when she broke her foot, they gave her all the support and encouragement she needed.

Jill knew how lucky she was to have them. So it was a little sad to think about going back to Denver to train. Still, Jill knew she wanted that more than anything.

"You guys are the best friends anyone ever had," Jill said suddenly. "And no matter what happens today, I know we all skated really well."

Haley gave Jill a quick squeeze. "Thanks," she said softly.

"Thanks, Jill," Nikki echoed. "But when will they tell us how we did?" she added anxiously. "I'm so nervous! But you really did look great, Jill. I'd be surprised if they don't take you and Amber. And Haley and Patrick for pairs," Nikki finished.

Amber! In the excitement of her audition, Jill had almost forgotten Amber. Now it all came flooding back. Jill knew that the younger girl had made a good impression, too. There was only one Clara role, but, as Nikki had reminded her, there were at least two good skaters to fill it. It all came down to what the scouts thought.

Jill glanced again in their direction. The three were huddled in a conference, going over their notes. There seemed to be some sort of disagreement among them.

Please, please let me be chosen, Jill repeated to herself. This is my big chance.

After a few more minutes, the scouts called Kathy and Dan over. Again there was some lively discussion, but they were so far away that no one could hear a word. Jill noticed Danielle trying to get as close as possible to them without being noticed. But Kathy saw her and waved her away.

Danielle came quickly back.

"Well?" Jill asked. "Could you hear anything?"

"No," she answered, shaking her head. "Sorry."

Martina joined Jill, Nikki, Haley, and Danielle. "Hi," she said quietly. "I'm keeping my fingers crossed for you guys."

Jill put an arm around Martina. "We're all waiting together," she said. Martina gave her a grateful smile.

Haley tossed her head. "I can't stand it!" she exploded.

"Haley, what's wrong?" Jill asked her in surprise. "You did great. Why are you so upset?"

Haley hesitated. "Don't take this the wrong way, Jill—you skated great today. But I can't stop thinking about Tori! She's good, too. If she hadn't quit, she would be waiting with us. She should have a chance at the Clara role. I just wish she had auditioned!" Haley looked down at her feet, embarrassed in front of Jill.

"It's okay, Haley. I know how you feel," Jill assured her. "Tori *is* a great skater." Jill knew she was the better skater technically, but in auditions like these, technique didn't count for everything. Tori had good looks and a strong personality on the ice. The scouts might have preferred Tori to Jill. Now Jill—and Tori—would never know.

"Tori's been part of our group for so long," Jill continued. "It feels wrong somehow to be here without her."

Had Tori really left Silver Blades for good? Jill shook her head. It was unbelievable. The Tori she knew could never give up all she had accomplished. She was too dedicated to her skating.

Part of Jill still hoped Tori would just show up and go for it. But it was a little late for that now.

"Well, there's something else," Haley admitted. She

looked right at Jill. "You know that we're the last club to audition for the scouts. If they haven't found a Clara yet, they could choose one of us. With Tori gone, that leaves you and Amber. And that doesn't seem fair. It should have been you or Tori. I mean, Amber just got here!"

Jill dropped her eyes. It was exactly what she had been thinking, though she would never say it out loud. Martina reached over and took Jill's hand. For a moment everyone was silent.

"What *is* taking so long?" Nikki finally burst out. She looked as nervous as Jill felt. "Are those scouts going to argue all day? Are they ever going to tell us anything?"

As the anticipation grew Jill was practically jumping up and down with excitement. The longer the scouts argued, the more nervous Jill felt. She was used to being judged in competitions where she learned her marks soon after she skated. This long delay was torture.

Martina shook her head. "I'm starting to wonder if anyone in Silver Blades will be picked at all!"

From the looks on the others' faces, Martina wasn't the only one wondering that. Jill caught herself twisting her bracelet around and around nervously.

But finally the group conference between the scouts and the Silver Blades coaches broke up. Kathy motioned to the waiting group.

"Come over here, everybody," Kathy called. "The scouts are ready now."

Jill sighed with relief. Haley and Nikki actually cheered out loud. They all bent to put on their skate guards. Then they hurried to where Kathy and the scouts were sitting.

Kathy beamed at them. She leaned close to the group, as excited as Jill had ever seen her. "First off, I want you all to know that you skated well," she said. "I'm proud of each one of you." Kathy paused and took a deep breath.

"But here's the biggest news," she continued. "The scouts tell me they've found their Clara—right here in Silver Blades!"

Jill felt her stomach do a flip-flop. Someone from Silver Blades was Clara. Someone had really been chosen for the plum role. Someone was about to get the chance of a lifetime.

But who?

Don't miss the exciting conclusion of this two-part series. Read Silver Blades #14, *Nutcracker on Ice.*

#5: The Perfect Pair

Nikki Simon and Alex Beekman are the perfect pair on the ice. But off the ice there's a big problem. Suddenly Alex is sending Nikki gifts and asking her out on dates. Nikki wants to be Alex's partner in pairs but not his girlfriend. Will she lose Alex when she tells him? Can Nikki's friends in Silver Blades find a way to save her friendship with Alex *and* her skating career?

#6: Skating Camp

Summer's here, and Jill Wong can't wait to join her best friends from Silver Blades at skating camp. It's going to be just like old times. But things have changed since Jill left Silver Blades to train at a famous ice academy. Tori and Danielle are spending all their time with another skater, Haley Arthur, and Nikki has a big secret that she won't share with anyone. Has Jill lost her best friends forever?

#7: The Ice Princess

Tori's favorite skating superstar, Elyse Taylor, is in town, and she's staying with Tori! When Elyse promises to teach Tori her famous spin, Tori's sure they'll become the best of friends. But Elyse isn't the sweet champion everyone thinks she is. And she's out to make real problems for Tori!

#8: Rumors at the Rink

Haley can't believe it—Kathy Bart, her favorite coach in the whole world, is quitting Silver Blades! Haley's sure it's all her fault. Why didn't she listen when everyone told her to stop playing practical jokes on Kathy? With Kathy gone, Haley knows she'll never win the next big competition. She has to make Kathy change her mind—no matter what. But will Haley's secret plan work?

#9: Spring Break

Jill is home from the Ice Academy, and everyone is treating her like a star. And she loves it! It's like a dream come true—especially when she meets cute, fifteen-year-old Ryan McKensey. He's so fun and cool—and he happens to be her number-one fan! The only problem is that he doesn't understand what it takes to be a professional athlete. Jill doesn't want to ruin her chances with such a great guy. But will dating Ryan destroy her future as an Olympic skater?

#10: Center Ice

It's gold medal time for Tori—she just knows it! The next big competition is coming up, and Tori has a winning routine. Now all she needs is that fabulous skating dress her mother promised her! But Mrs. Carsen doesn't seem to be interested in Tori's skating anymore—not since she started dating a new man in town. When Mrs. Carsen tells Tori she's not going to the competition, Tori decides enough is enough! She has a plan that will change everything—forever!

#11: A Surprise Twist

Danielle's on top of the world! All her hard work at the rink has paid off. She's good. Very good. And Dani's new English teacher, Ms. Howard, says she has a real flair for writing—she might even be the best writer in her class. Trouble is, there's a big skating competition coming up—and a writing contest. Dani's stumped. Her friends and family are counting on her to skate her best. But Ms. Howard is counting on her to write a winning story. How can Dani choose between skating and her new passion?

#12: The Winning Spirit

A group of Special Olympics skaters is on the way to Seneca Hills! The skaters are going to pair up with the Silver Blades members in a minicompetition. Everyone in Silver Blades

thinks Ni... ...rt-
ner is Ca... ...est
visiting s... ...ea
of skatin... ...he-
thing . . .

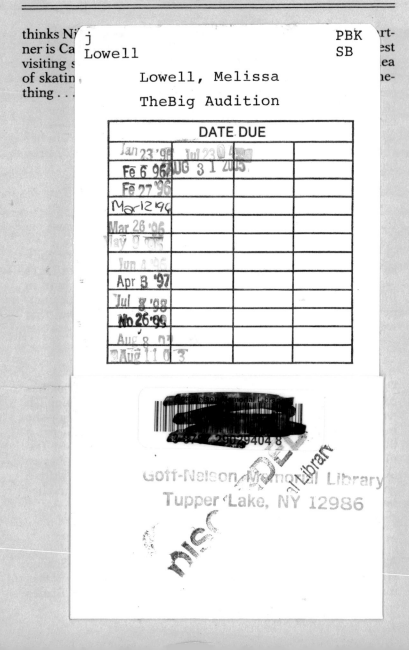